Sherlock Holmes
and the
Morphine Gambit

Jason Cooke

A Sherlock Holmes murder mystery
First published in 2009
under the Breese Books imprint by
The Irregular Special Press
for Baker Street Studios Ltd
Endeavour House
170 Woodland Road, Sawston
Cambridge CB22 3DX, UK

ISBN: 1-901091-33-3 (10 digit)
ISBN: 978-1-901091-33-5 (13 digit)

Cover Concept: Antony J. Richards

Cover Illustration: Looking along the coast from Cromer to Overstrand. Sea Marge
can be clearly seen on top of the cliff with Holmes and Watson on the beach below
looking out towards the *Misty Jane*. From an original watercolour by Nikki Sims

Typeset in 8/11/20pt Palatino

From the archives of the late
John H. Watson M.D.

Preface

O f all the many sensitive affairs in which my friend Sherlock Holmes has been involved during the course of his long and celebrated career, I can recall only half a dozen cases which have involved issues of such moment as to give rise to a publicity ban of no less than fifty years. The adventure of 1907 I have chronicled under the title of *The St. Petersburg Deception* was one such, as was the case of the supposedly insoluble *Shanghai Sorcerer Mystery* of 1900, but the clandestine investigation which absorbed the master detective so completely during February 1912 was at the forefront of these affairs due to national security implications of the gravest nature. To the handful of British officials who were witness to those exciting and extraordinary events, the case which I can finally put to the reader came guardedly to be referred to as *The Morphine Gambit*. The government of the day left me in no doubt that publication of this story was not in the public interest, so common-sense and Holmes' own rigorous strictures of sensitivity and secrecy have lead me, as his biographer, to record this account and hold it in the vaults of Cox & Co. for the requisite period until such time as future researchers may gain access to my papers.

Chapter One

Intruders in the Night

I remember well the first turn of the wheel of events that lead to one of the most intriguing espionage and counter-espionage adventures this country can have seen in this or any other century. It began, like so many of my other adventures with Holmes, in so innocuous a fashion. My diary informs me that the date was Saturday 17th February 1912. I remember peering out from the French windows of my study, whence I had retired at mid-morning to digest a full English breakfast, and regarding with no friendly eye the unremitting gloom of a typical February morning. The tiniest shoots of a few early daffodils could be seen bravely fighting their way above the mud of the garden, and the winter survivors among my clematis clung doggedly to their trellises, but heavy rain drummed on the patio and the birds were strangely absent. I could identify but three metaphorical rays of sunshine in the morning's proceedings; the first was the coal fire that burned merrily in my study hearth, the second was the pot of real Brazilian coffee from which I had just poured my second cup, and the third was a telegram from Mr Sherlock Holmes that lay opened upon my bureau. This item comprised the sum total of my incoming mail for that morning, and on the face of it was unremarkable, the language short and terse as always.

> ARRIVING VICTORIA 12:50 TRAIN. WILL JOIN YOU FOR TEA. DINNER AT SIMPSONS. TRUST YOU ARE RECOVERED FROM INFLUENZA. SH

The text of this missive may have been unremarkable but the event to which it referred, a visit to London by Sherlock Holmes, was very remarkable indeed. Latterly his visits to town had become so infrequent that I had not seen him for a good twelve months, and, as he had made a habit of always staying with me during his trips to the Capital, I could safely conclude that his last visit had been over a year ago. I was simultaneously pleased at the prospect of seeing my old friend once more, and vaguely intrigued as to what business he had which could be so important as to necessitate a personal visit. I pondered this question briefly, and then took up the telegram once more. Certain features of his correspondence never changed, I reflected. His period of notice before descending upon my house was invariably less than a day, I noted a little ruefully. He always made reference to Simpson's, that well-known restaurant on the Strand that we had patronised so often during our sojourn at Baker Street, and to which he still felt a sentimental attachment. And he usually made reference to some little item that he knew would intrigue or mystify me, in this instance, how he could possibly have known of my mild case of flu earlier in the month was a source of complete bafflement to me, as we had not entered into any correspondence since Christmas. I made a mental note to question my friend over this matter and prepared myself for the inevitably simple answer delivered with the usual devastating logic.

The pleasing news of Holmes' impending visit caused me to turn away from the window and gaze fondly over at the locked cabinet in the corner of the study, which contained tangible reminders of my times with the great detective. The bottom three drawers were crammed with case papers, notes, diagrams, chronological listings and indexes, and the original copies of those investigations that I had already written up and placed before the public. The upper half of the cabinet, a glass-shelved display case protected by two locked glass doors, contained various relics and souvenirs from some of the detective's most notable cases. He, in his absent-minded manner, had sought to dispose of many articles of interest in a great clearout just before his retirement to Sussex, and it was left to me to salvage these artefacts before they were lost forever. I added them to my own small but growing collection of memorabilia that I am confident any student of his remarkable career will find fascinating in years to come.

Even then, before the labelling and arranging of the many items making up my miniature museum was complete, two out of three shelves were replete with souvenirs. The business card of the formidable Dr Trevelyan from the case of *The Missing Three-Quarter* was on display, as was an unmarked bottle that contained the lethal African potion from the case of the *Devil's Foot*. I had preserved one of the letters from the case of *The Dancing Men*, with its unusual and enigmatic cipher, and I suppressed a shudder as I viewed again the polished wooden dart, loosed from a blowpipe during a frantic chase up the Thames, which had come within inches of ending Sherlock Holmes' burgeoning career at the end of *The Sign of Four*.

I could not suppose that Holmes' visit today would herald the sort of adventure that had given rise to the contents of this cabinet, indeed I was not aware that he had taken up any case for years. At this time I was long withdrawn from general practice and enjoying the early years of my retirement at my rooms in Queen Anne Street, although in truth I was not yet so settled that I did not still harbour designs for a permanent move out of the Metropolis (my first since I was discharged from the army in 1887). The changes that Edwardian England had brought to London – the increased tempo of life, the noise and fresh forms of pollutants emanating from the growing numbers of motorcars on the streets, and the tangible new uncertainty in the national mood, naturally to be felt strongest in the nation's Capital – all these factors combined to lead me to consider an exodus to the country where the pace of life is slower and the pressure of world affairs encroaches less forcefully.

I had in fact already conducted some gentle research in the Home Counties as to a possible relocation befitting an old warhorse going out to pasture, and had my eye on the Sussex town of Rye. The town seemed ideal, within reach of London if the withdrawal from city life was so painful as to require relief of the symptoms by frequent return visits, yet benefiting from south coast weather patterns and architecturally appealing with a rich smuggling history. I envisaged pleasant lunchtimes spent at the Mermaid Inn consuming real ale and hearty lunches. My one concern was the close proximity to my old friend in his bee-keeping retreat on the Sussex Downs; on the one hand it would be the perfect opportunity to see more of Holmes, but I had no desire to dog his footsteps now that the career with which I had once been associated was well and truly behind him, and I feared his reaction when he learned of my interest. Nevertheless, his impending visit of the afternoon would provide the ideal opportunity to tackle him on the subject. Before preparing for his visit, however, I spent half an hour with the remaining contents of my coffee pot and the morning edition of *The Times.*

The new problems and uncertainties bedevilling English society since the coming of the Edwardian era were graphically illustrated in every article on the front page. I personally had every sympathy with the cause of the female vote, but the methods and activities of the more militant Suffragettes were disturbing and socially divisive. The supposed failure of Prime Minister Asquith's Liberal policies governing social and economic reform had led to unprecedented strikes among the workforce of the rail and coal industries. Relations with Germany were at a most delicate stage; international tensions with ourselves and the French had only just subsided following the Moroccan crisis of the previous year, the mission of War Secretary Haldane to limit German naval expansion had failed just this month, and there was growing speculation in the national newspapers that the Germans were covertly supplying arms to Irish extremists on both sides of the Home Rule for Ireland debate. Things were very different from the settled imperial supremacy of the last years of Queen Victoria. I shook my head in trepidation as to where all this might lead, folded my newspaper, and went off to prepare the guest bedroom for Holmes.

At twenty minutes to five I answered a distinct knock at the door, and there, clutching a large valise and sheltering beneath an enormous umbrella from which the rain cascaded, stood a smiling Sherlock Holmes.

"My dear Holmes," I greeted him, shaking his hand warmly, "come in out of this lamentable weather."

I scrutinised him carefully as I spoke, noting a few more lines around the eyes than when I saw him last, but his gaze was as bright and piercing as ever and I could not discern any addition of weight to his whip-lean countenance. He stood, dripping water onto the wooden tiles of my hall from his overcoat and smart three-piece suit, and continued to smile mischievously.

"Well, Watson, do I pass muster?"

I acquiesced that he did indeed look well.

"That is most fortunate," he cried, "and my enquiry to you in my recent telegram as to the state of *your* health was no idle pleasantry, as I require your services forthwith for a short trip to East Anglia."

"Of course," I replied, momentarily forgetting to query this odd announcement, "but how were you aware that I had been unwell at all?"

I found I was addressing the last question to his retreating back. Having divested himself of his outer garments onto my coat rack he strode towards the withdrawing room, from whence his voice came booming back.

"I understand you are shortly to enter the property market in Sussex, Watson. I should purchase in Rye immediately if I were you, as properties seldom become available in that attractive town, particularly ones within the financial range of a half–pay surgeon. I would appreciate having you closer to hand. By the way, do you still keep any of my pipes; I seem to have left all of mine at home."

Seated comfortably in front of a fire with a pipe of tobacco in hand, pleasantries were observed before Holmes began to offer explanations.

"As you must be aware, it is now nine years since I formally retired to the county of Sussex. Knowing me as you do, you must surely be aware that I have traversed the county during explorations on foot and by horse and coach. Bearing in mind my former career, is it not inconceivable to you that I would waste opportunities to make contact with those in points around the county who may be in a position or of a mind to pass on to me information which may be of interest? Obviously my efforts in this regard were helped by my small reputation as a retired private detective of note, and I soon found that I had many prospective informers stretching the length and breadth of the county. Thus when I hear from a travelling salesman that my old friend Watson, who was once as much of a household name as myself, has made enquiries with property agents in Rye while at the same time looking distinctly under the weather, it did not take me long to deduce both the nature of your business in Rye and the fact that your were suffering from an ailment which was severe enough to make its mark upon your countenance but not severe enough to confine you to bed. I remembered from our shared Baker Street experiences how susceptible you are to influenza during the closing stages of the winter season, a feature of the constitutional weakness caused by injuries from your Afghan campaigns, and my simple deductive chain was complete."

"Amazing," I replied, marvelling at my friend's ability to garner information even when away from it all in such a rural retreat. "And now what brings you to town, and what business awaits us in East Anglia?"

"A request from Mycroft, is the answer to the first part of your question," answered Holmes bluntly. I had not seen or heard of Holmes' brother Mycroft for many a year, and assumed he had retired.

"He is retained by the Government in a consultative capacity," advised Holmes. "I received a telegram at home early this morning in which he requested my presence forthwith in Whitehall ... hence the suit ... as he wished to discuss with me a sensitive matter of Governmental importance. I made up my mind to attend, as I am between projects at home; have not seen you, friend Watson, for a good while; and because a summons from Mycroft is so rare as to generally demand attendance. Following his telegram I spoke to him in London on the telephone from my local village post office, and he assured me that if I were unwilling to come up to town for an interview, he would make the trip down to Sussex in order to brief me in person. As you know Watson, Mycroft has the most capacious and analytical mind in the kingdom, but the greatness of his mental condition is compensated for by his utter distaste for any form of physical exertion. For him to make such a promise, then, and on a Saturday of all days, when, as a general principle, senior civil servants are most definitely *not* to be found at work, was evidence that something serious was afoot. I sent word to you as soon as I had spoken to him, and then came straight up to town. I have just left Mycroft in Whitehall."

"And the case?" I enquired. The maid entered the room with a tray of tea and stoked up the fire. Holmes waited until she had poured the tea and left the room before replying.

"I was on the verge of addressing the second part of your original question. But we have less than an hour to spare. Time is pressing if we are to be of use in the matter. It is well that your maid provided us with such a plentiful array of cakes with our tea, as I am afraid we will have to forego Simpson's. We must take the seven o'clock train from Liverpool Street to Cromer in Norfolk and trust in the generosity of our host, Sir Edward Muster, to provide us with a late supper. A swift departure is no inconvenience to you?"

"By no means," I replied, my curiosity awakened.

"Well then. Have you heard of Sir Edward Muster?"

I had to confess that I had not.

"An hour spent in the reference rooms of the British Library furnished me with a potted *curriculum vitae* of this gentleman. Sir Edward can be found in *Who's Who* chiefly on the strength of his prominent position within the City of London. Hailing from a well-established German family whose business empire centres on banking, textiles and pharmaceuticals, Sir Edward came to London in 1891 as an emissary of the family firm. He has, however, clearly inherited the business acumen of his forefathers. If all I hear and read is to be believed, he has extended the family empire into the British banking sector and used this country as a base to expand his business interests elsewhere in Europe. On account of his successes, family connections in Germany, and, I am told, a genuinely charismatic personality, he moves in exalted political circles in London and has many highly placed friends ... these include no less than the King himself and also the Prime Minister, Herbert Asquith. He was made a Privy Councillor in 1908. He is married, to Lady Stefanie Muster, but has no children. To complete my sketch, he is also well-known as a philanthropist who has donated considerable sums of money to artistic and charitable foundations in the East End of London."

"How does Mycroft regard him?" I interjected.

"Very highly. He maintains that he is man of considerable integrity and noble character. Mycroft met him some years ago at a reception at the German embassy. The two got along very well and I understand Mycroft used to lunch with him at the Diogenes club. It is partly out of concern for his old friend that Mycroft has urged us to lend our resources to assisting him during his present predicament. I say partly, because there are perhaps weightier issues involved. Due to his Anglo-German background, the circles in which he moves and his considerable reputation, I understand that Sir Edward has in the past been used in an unofficial capacity as an ambassador in certain delicate missions to the Kaiser. Given the strained state of relations between ourselves and Germany at the present time, not to mention the numerous other political issues affecting continental stability at home and abroad, it is clear that the British Government would place considerable stock in safeguarding such a prominent and valuable personality."

"And something has happened that may compromise this security?" I queried.

Holmes rose, and, in the manner I remembered so well from the past, began striding up and down the room.

"Two incidents. Sir Edward has a property in Belgravia from where he conducts much of his London business, but lately he has been spending more and more time at a capacious residence called Sea Marge he has had built in the well-to-do village of Overstrand, near Cromer. Last night an insomniac servant surprised intruders as they slipped out of Sir Edward's study via a pair of forced French windows. Despite immediately raising the alarm the two nighthawks escaped into the gardens. The door locks had apparently been expertly forced, in what is referred to in today's modern parlance as a 'professional job', I believe. Sir Edward and his family were in residence at the time and they remain in Norfolk awaiting our arrival. At the same time his house in Belgravia was ransacked and the house contents left in disarray. In this case, however, the few servants living on site, in adjoining rooms, apparently heard nothing."

"Was anything taken, Holmes? What do you think they were after?"

"Sir Edward's servants in London spent this morning clearing up and taking an inventory. Some family silver is missing and one or two works of art. The lock on the study door had been disabled and Sir Edward's papers and small reference library had been rifled; documents were strewn haphazardly all over the floor. In Norfolk, Sir Edward believes that nothing has been taken. On the accuracy of all this information we shall reserve judgement, my dear Watson, until we have had a chance to examine the evidence firsthand."

"But you have a theory?"

Holmes smiled indulgently. "I see that your advancing years have deprived you of recalling even the most basic of rules under which I used to operate. It is highly dangerous to theorise until in full possession of the facts. I have an idea, and this idea leads me to conclude that the starting point for our investigation should be Norfolk and not London. It is, however, patently obvious that these break-ins have caused something of a stir in official quarters, as Scotland Yard detectives have been assigned to the Belgravia case and I understand that Special Branch officers are already on hand in Norfolk assisting the local people. Privately, Mycroft has confided in me that he fears that Sir Edward's life is in danger from extremist German or pro-German assassins, who want him dead and thus the removal of his benevolent influence on Anglo-German relations. I am not convinced; if that were the case these desperate men could simply have killed Sir Edward in his bed last night."

"The idea may have merit," I ventured. "Perhaps after rifling the contents of his study to discover the state of his public and private affairs, this was precisely their intention? Perhaps they struck, with lethal intent, against both of Sir Edward's properties on the same night in order to guard against his being absent from one or the other?"

Holmes shook his head thoughtfully. "Hmm. One must remain open to all possibilities. I must confess the prospect of betrayal, motivated by personal profit, by a trusted member, or members, of Sir Edward's household has crossed *my* mind, whether crudely engineering the theft of Sir Edward's valuable property by ruthless persons as yet unknown, or pursuing an even darker design."

"Darker ... ?" I queried.

"Tssk, Watson. Blackmail! Both raids appear to display evidence of interest in the contents of Sir Edwards' studies. It may be that someone is prepared to go to considerable lengths to secure certain papers or other ... interesting documentation on such a public figure. We may have to employ the utmost tact in raising this possibility with our host of this evening."

"In any event," Holmes went on, "Mycroft has asked me to make some inquiries as an impartial observer and submit a full report to him. I naturally hoped I could rely on your assistance and besides, a few days in the fresh sea air will do wonders for that failing constitution of yours. Therefore if you will now be so good as to pack clothes and toiletries sufficient for a few days in the field, we can then proceed directly to Liverpool Street. I can further update you during the journey. Oh, and Watson, please remember to pack your old service revolver."

"Certainly," I said, putting down my teacup and standing up. "One final point, Holmes; why do we commence our enquiries in Overstrand ahead of Belgravia? You did mention that you had an idea in this regard?"

"I do," replied my friend. "It is my current belief that the key to this mystery will be found on the coast rather than in town."

"On what grounds?"

Holmes gazed at the ceiling thoughtfully. "Simply this. The Norfolk raid seems to bear the hallmarks of men who knew what they were looking for."

His gaze fell to the grandfather clock in the corner of the withdrawing room. "Hurry, Watson, pack swiftly and let us go," he murmured softly.

Chapter Two

Overstrand

Half an hour later saw us hailing a horse-drawn cab, a declining species with the coming of the motorcar, and making the short trip to Liverpool Street station. The noise and fumes of the motorcars thronging the streets were an unpleasant distraction, but I could not gainsay that the increasing number of these new-fangled machines on the road had resulted in smoother surfaces, and hence a more comfortable journey for ourselves. We had little difficulty orientating ourselves at Liverpool Street station and as always I found myself marvelling at the huge domed roofs, criss-crossed with iron girders and supported by towering columns, that comprised the structure of this great terminus. Large enough to cater for the thousands of City businessmen from Greater London, Essex, and beyond that flooded into, and out of, the city during the working week, even at this late hour numerous individuals in city pinstripe and bowler hats were hurrying to catch their connections home. Uniformed porters were everywhere and the loud blast of steam whistles filled the air.

Holmes and I located our service, the *Cromer Express*, and we had barely got ourselves settled in a first class carriage before the great train was pulling out of the station. Despite the season, our carriage was busy with families, complete with servants, animals and luggage, who appeared to be making a weekend departure for the coast. I remarked on this to Holmes, who gave the following comment.

"You must be aware that the town of Cromer became fashionable among the genteel and well-to-do in the second half of the last century as a picturesque seaside resort within reasonably easy reach of London. I understand that the Victorian leisure pastime of sea bathing first became popular there. The demands of the holidaymakers of the last century resulted in the establishment of a fast and efficient railway service to convey wealthy families and their servants from London to the coast in comfort. It is such a service that we are at this moment availing ourselves of, and I am certain that an extended weekend break remains the purpose of the bulk of our fellow travellers. So popular had Cromer become by the turn of the century that many affluent gentlemen built or purchased second homes in the town or surrounding villages. One of these is the village of Overstrand, not two miles from the town."

"I do perceive, Watson," continued Holmes, lowering his voice slightly "that the angst in Whitehall has been exacerbated by the number of wealthy men of influence who, in addition to Sir Edward, have also chosen Overstrand as the location for their holiday villas. I understand from Mycroft that the banker Lord Hillingdon has bought a property in this quiet and picturesque village, as has the wealthy iron and steel merchant Sir Daniel Everard, knighted for services to Imperial commerce. Lord Battersea, owner of large tracts of land in south London also has a summer residence in Overstrand, designed by no less than Lutyens, the well-known Dutch architect. A veritable coterie of the great and the good, eh, Watson? Little wonder Special Branch detectives are involved. Let's see if this old dog can still run with the young pups!"

The powerful locomotive transported us swiftly across East Anglia, crossing the counties of Essex, Suffolk and Norfolk in under three hours, and we arrived at Cromer Beach station at five minutes to ten. The rain which had so beset us in London let up as we travelled, and this and the moonlit night allowed me some glimpses of the beautiful East Anglian countryside, with its splendid churches built from the profits of weaving and textiles during the Middle Ages, and its quilted patchwork of fields under crop. Holmes and I were met at the station by Sir Edward's representative driver, and as we strode outside I fully expected to see a horse and trap or small coach. However the sight that greeted us was a small *Model T* Ford, the archetypal American mass-produced family motorcar. Rumours of the durability and economy of this small vehicle had reached us in England, but I had yet to see one on this side of the Atlantic. I remarked on this to Sir Edward's driver, Bishop by name, as the Cromer porter loaded our luggage into the back of the motorcar.

"Sir Edward has great business foresight and is a great believer in the emerging technologies," he replied. "As for motorcars, well, he has two others in Norfolk alone, a British Wolsey and a Daimler."

Our driver was a local man, and, by way of introduction to this part of the Norfolk coast, drove us up through the centre of Cromer before turning off towards the village of Overstrand, a two mile trip up a gradual incline skirting fields and pastureland bordered by woodland. Holmes began a steady cross-examination of our guide as we travelled, his fame ensuring an eager stream of replies, and soon he was gleaning information on many aspects of Sir Edward's life from his business and travel affairs to his domestic arrangements.

"So let me understand you, Bishop. In this country alone Sir Edward possesses residences in Belgravia in London and here in Overstrand, and a suite of offices in High Holborn?"

"That's right, Mr Holmes. 'Course Mr Muster is a wealthy man with other houses and business assets in Europe, particularly in Germany."

"Any areas in particular?" my colleague returned.

"Frankfurt, I believe, and Darmstadt ... and Berlin of course. I know he has considerable banking interests in Holland, as well."

"Has he been abroad recently?"

"He was at a conference in Holland earlier in the year and then had a few days in Germany on business. Most of January, this was. Sir Edward, Lady Muster, along with his closest advisors and staff. Most of us who work at his English properties were given time on leave."

Holmes turned and muttered an aside to me. "Why not raid his properties in January, then, with a skeleton staff on duty both here and in London and a lesser chance of discovery at either end?"

While the conversation between Holmes and Bishop was in progress, I began to familiarise myself with the immediate area.

Our little motorcar seemed incongruous in the town of Cromer as we weaved between the odd horse and cart, still about despite the lateness of the hour, and pedestrians crisscrossing the main street. We drove along the short illuminated promenade and it was all too clear that the original fishing community was gradually being overcome by the demands of the fashionable holiday resort. Stretching out to sea from the promenade was the new Cromer pier, and a row of grand hotels, towering brick edifices with names of Victorian resonance such as The Grand or the Clifton, provided a backdrop to the short but sweeping avenue on which we travelled. Nevertheless away from this main route, in the alleys which led down to the beach and at the far end of the promenade, the odd fisherman could be seen working on nets and pots by the light of a guttering fish-oil lamp, casting eerie shadows over the shacks and colourful crab boats and small trawlers drawn up at the top of the beach.

The drive to the village of Overstrand led past Cromer golf course, of which several holes were perched close to the cliff-edge, and past the whitewashed lighthouse.

"The waters off this coast are deadly," advised our driver grimly. "Shallow and treacherous. The currents, shoals and sandbars have claimed so many victims over the years that the last century saw the beginning of our lifeboat service and the building of two lighthouses, here and at Haisbro', further along the coast. Lord Nelson lost one of his warships off Haisbro' in 1801; the *Invincible*, she went down with the loss of around four hundred men. Not that the sandbanks offshore bother Winston Churchill, however. He spends his summers on holiday in Overstrand and, since he was made First Sea Lord last year, has taken to making the trip up from London in the Admiralty yacht. Local fishermen bring him and his family and retainers ashore and then they simply walk up wooden steps from the beach to the village."

"It is entirely possible, then, to launch and land a small

boat from the foot of Overstrand cliffs?" interjected Holmes.

"Entirely possible," said Bishop, "although if you are enquiring with regard to the events of last night, Mr Holmes, we experienced high winds and heavy rain here and I reckon all local boats would have been in port."

"And yet you cannot be certain?" my colleague persisted.

"Not certain, no," replied Bishop, in a tone that suggested otherwise. "Here, we've just time for me to quickly show you the beach before we reach Sea Marge."

Overstrand appeared, even at night, to be an exceedingly attractive village, complete with those four village staples; a comely medieval church; a public house – the White Horse; a village shop; and a post office. Two narrow lanes converged on a small promenade, which overlooked a drop of seventy foot from the cliff edge down to a stretch of empty beach directly below us. In the distance could be heard the roar of the surf. From this promenade a track wound its way gracefully down to the beach, from whence the villages' handful of fishermen would launch their craft. In the village the lanes were lined with flint cottages sporting narrow windows and whitewashed walls, some of which appeared to be tucked away behind trees and wooden fences. Against the moonlit skyline a tall dovecote, or folly, towered over the tree line, evidently a feature of some mansion set in extensive private grounds. An owl hooted.

"The Pleasaunce, Lord Battersea's place," commented Bishop by way of explanation. We passed Pear Tree Cottage, a small brick and flint chalet set back from the road behind a small lawn where Mr Churchill spent his holidays, before turning left past the post office and the public house and on to Sea Marge.

Despite the lateness of the hour, Sea Marge was brightly lit as we arrived. I confess I was taken aback by the grandeur of the mansion, which had only been completed and made fully habitable the previous autumn. I had learnt from Holmes that Sir Edward had acquired a shell of a property and invested and reconstructed heavily to build his ideal holiday villa. The house was slightly set back from the road in a shallow depression, partially hidden from casual observers by beautifully manicured hedges. Even at that time of night I could appreciate the sweeping L-shaped expanse of the property and its outbuildings, which, in mock-Elizabethan style, featured whitewashed walls interspersed with seasoned timbers along its length. At the far left of the estate was a large redbrick outhouse that, Bishop informed us, Sir Edward used to store his collection of automobiles. A very short drive led to the main entrance, covered by a beautifully carved arched porch, where Bishop halted our conveyance and began removing our luggage.

Holmes and I dismounted and began to move through into the hall, whereupon we were challenged by a burly police sergeant sporting a rain cape. He seemed to materialise from the shadows outside the porch. On establishing our credentials the policeman gave a respectful nod to my companion and bade us move on into the hall and thence to the right into the smoking room.

My impressions of elegant luxury at Sea Marge were further reinforced within. Oak panelled corridors led off a wide spacious hall, itself boasting crystal chandeliers and Delft wall tiles. Seated comfortably by Sir Edward's butler, Hawkins, in the smoking room, I noted the fine furniture, the elegant fireplace that currently harboured a roaring fire, and the beech panelling hung with drapes that lined the walls. A bar area contained a selection of port and fine wines that would not have disgraced a club in St. James' or Pall Mall. Diamond-paned, arched windows gave views to seaward, while the nautical theme (so beloved of the owner-builder, as I later discovered), was further promoted by a series of round oak windows which gave the appearance of portholes, and in the fact that the house was built square on to the sea, no more than one hundred yards away at the bottom of the cliff, so that from all the windows of the seaward side, from the ground to the second storey, one had a perfect view of the ocean. Although I could but dimly see it, the seaward side of the house abutted a charming patio sporting Romanesque statues, and sloping away to the cliff edge a hundred yards distant were ornate gardens that Bishop had already mentioned to us during the journey from the railway station.

The abiding initial impression that I gained from Sea Marge was one of the considerable wealth and power of an influential Edwardian gentleman. Within five minutes of the arrival of Holmes and myself this impression was confirmed, as Sir Edward Muster came striding into the hall accompanied by his wife, Lady Muster. Sir Edward, a tall man wearing a cravat and smoking jacket, looked every inch a member of the upper classes, as did his wife, Lady Stefanie, a regal and aristocratic lady. If their recent experience had told on their nerves, it did not show. Sir Edward clutched Holmes' business card as he moved towards us. Behind our hosts followed a short, rotund man in a business suit, and a non-descript man sporting a moustache wearing a light overcoat and wool scarf. My colleague measured up the newcomers in an instant.

"My dear Sir Edward," said Holmes, rising, "and Lady Muster, allow me to offer my sympathies for this recent intrusion into your privacy and the shock involved. I am

Sherlock Holmes and this is my colleague, Dr Watson."

"I recognised you instantly," smiled Sir Edward, "for you look very much like Mycroft despite the dissimilarities in, er, physique. Good evening to you too, Doctor. The exploits of the two of you are somewhat legendary, but I believe it is you we have to thank for recording your adventures for public consumption!" His eyes sparkled merrily. "Now that I have the legendary Sherlock Holmes on the case we shall soon have this business cleared up."

Holmes, however, was grave.

"Sir Edward, I believe I should be frank with you. You are a peer of the realm actively involved in business and politics; in short, a prominent and important personality, exposed to the public eye. As such your friends and colleagues within the British Government do not, regretfully, believe that this is an episode that can be regarded lightly. As a friend, Mycroft is concerned for the wellbeing of you, your family, and your household. Without wishing to resort to wanton self-flattery, it is a measure of the severity with which the British Government views this incident that they have called upon me to offer my assistance in any way I can. Whitehall is taking this matter very seriously. Any small investigative ability I have garnered in my years as a private detective is entirely at your service in solving this mystery."

"An offer that is gratefully acknowledged not only by me and my wife but, also, no doubt, by Inspector Jackson of the Metropolitan Police Special Branch." Here Sir Edward indicated the man standing behind him in the overcoat.

"A great pleasure to be working alongside you, Mr Holmes," advised Jackson. "I must speak with you shortly to bring you up to date on the case. I have just finished discussing the issues of the day with Sir Edward and Lady Muster."

"And this is Mr Wilson, my business manager and personal secretary," added Sir Edward, almost as an afterthought.

The fourth person in the group, the short man in a business suit, nodded to us briefly. He wore small round glasses on his rounded face, and the combination seemed to bestow upon him an air of cunning, or of knowing a great deal which he chose to keep to himself.

"If you require anything at all during your stay just mention it to Wilson here and you shall have it," said Sir Edward. "With your permission, Mr Holmes, my wife and I will retire shortly as the events of the past twenty-four hours have been somewhat unsettling. Is there anything that you and your colleague require from me presently? I will of course have supper brought to you."

Holmes held up his hand and shook his head. "My questions can wait until tomorrow, Sir Edward, when I will take the opportunity to conduct a short interview with you and your wife" – here Holmes nodded and smiled at Lady Muster – "and also the other members of your household. I would however like to make a brief examination of your study before I turn in, and have a few words with Inspector Jackson."

"Of course," said Sir Edward, rising and shaking hands. "I'll leave you with Jackson here. Hawkins will bring you some supper shortly. Please help yourselves to cigars and brandy here in the smoking room." He smiled. "Until tomorrow, then." Lady Muster bade us goodnight with a tired smile and Wilson also departed. Jackson led us from the smoking room through an annex into Sir Edward's study, a small room sporting the beams and whitewash so typical of the exterior of the property. A pair of French windows were installed in the north wall that opened out onto the patio to which I referred earlier; the patio in turn led on to the gardens which stretched away to the cliff. It was these portals that the intruders of the night before had apparently used to effect their entry to, and exit from, the property. Directly facing us as we entered the study from the west was a writing bureau on which lay various pens and inks and a number of papers that looked as though they had been recently catalogued. A telephone was on a small stand next to the bureau, and a fine armchair sat in front of it. A small fireplace was situated in the south wall. A small bookcase and the odd local print upon the walls completed the picture.

My companion studied the room carefully. "In what state was the study found?" he asked Jackson.

"Remarkably undisturbed. Sir Edward advised me this morning that, with the exception of the writing bureau and its contents, there was no mess or signs of disruption. However, the locks on the French windows had been forced to facilitate access and a small lock on the writing bureau had also been picked. The intruders appear to have been in the process of rifling Sir Edward's papers when Wilson disturbed them and they fled."

"If the study was in a remarkably undisturbed condition then it may follow that the intruders did not have long to conduct their researches before they were disturbed," commented Holmes. "I see Sir Edward has catalogued these papers to see if any are missing," said Holmes, running his fingers over a sheaf of papers on the edge of the bureau. "I understand he believes nothing to have been taken?"

"That is correct. Sir Edward operates a very simple filing

system in his study, with folders divided and sub-divided alphabetically. Judging from the haphazard state of a few of his files the intruders clearly had the opportunity to begin a systematic analysis of his documentation, but were then interrupted. Sir Edward does not, however, feel that anything has been taken."

Holmes then turned his attention to the French windows. "I see that you have not had the lock repaired," he said, opening the door and inspecting the metalwork.

"No," replied Jackson, "we have a locksmith coming out specially tomorrow but we thought you would like a look at it first." Holmes peered at the lock. "A simple lock," he announced presently, "but the mechanism has been turned very efficiently with seemingly little damage to the lock. Sophisticated equipment would seem to have been involved. No fingerprints?"

Jackson shook his head. "None. We believe they wore gloves. The lock on the bureau was also picked very efficiently, with top-of-the-range needle skeleton keys I would suggest. Sophisticated lock-picking equipment, gloves, dark clothing, an efficient search method evident in the study; this was a professional operation, Mr Holmes."

"I am inclined to agree with you," murmured Holmes. "Did you get a good description of the intruders? You say Wilson, Sir Edward's personal secretary disturbed them?"

"Yes. He caught a glimpse of them by lamplight as they escaped out into the gardens. He confirmed they were dressed in dark clothing and were probably wearing gloves. The last supposition was confirmed by our forensic representative who identified some fibres caught on the wood on the door frame."

"Mycroft told me this morning that the intruders were

disturbed at around half-past one in the morning. Did Wilson explain what he was doing in Sir Edward's study at that time of night in the first place?"

"Yes." Here Jackson fumbled for a notebook. "He says that he had been unable to sleep and had got up to go downstairs and check the state of the fire in the grate in this, the study, hearth. Sir Edward has confirmed to us that he worked in here last night, retiring well after midnight, and had had a fire lit as it was such a foul evening. Apparently, and this is confirmed by other members of staff, this hearth is prone to belching out quantities of smoke and debris into the room when a fire is lit during very windy weather. Wilson in particular has, in the past, voiced his concerns that under such circumstances a spark could escape that could catch on fabric or woodwork. With such a storm raging, and unable to sleep, Wilson came down to check that the fire was safe."

"If Sir Edward only went to bed after midnight and Wilson surprised the intruders at half past one, it follows that they may have mounted a vigil outside in the wet. There were no traces of damp, or mud or suchlike, in the study?" queried Holmes.

Jackson shook his head.

"Hmm." Holmes studied an oil lamp sitting on the bureau, and stared at the fireplace. He turned.

"I think that will do for tonight. You have clearly got down to business in a most efficient manner, Inspector," Holmes smiled. Jackson nodded. "We were fortunate that the local constabulary had arrived on site immediately after the event and isolated the area. Myself and my team, when we arrived this morning, had a very warm scent on which to run."

"Is anyone on hand from the Norfolk police?" asked Holmes.

"Only Sergeant Walker, whom I believe challenged you outside; he is the sole representative from the Norfolk police. The Home Office has decreed that this investigation should be under the control of Scotland Yard. Inspector Cooper of the Norfolk Police relinquished authority to me this morning. I have three armed officers billeted here who will patrol these grounds until I deem it fit to remove them. In addition, my superior Chief Inspector Carlisle is due to arrive tomorrow with a further five members of our reserve." Jackson lowered his voice slightly. "The security up here in Overstrand is a pain. This break-in business is one thing, but there are so many members of the establishment to be found up here at any one time that in the long term it may be wise to establish a Special Branch department at Cromer. Take tomorrow night, for example. Sir Edward is hosting a dinner in this house at which will be present no less than Winston Churchill, First Lord of the Admiralty as you know, Sir Daniel Everard the steel magnate, and Lord Battersea."

"And Watson and myself," said Holmes smiling again. "It will be an excellent opportunity to mingle with the locals and perhaps glean some useful information."

Seated back in the smoking room and attacking plates of bread and cheese brought to us by Hawkins, Sir Edward's butler, Holmes asked Jackson if he had a theory with regards to the case in hand.

"We do. We are inclined against the idea of an opportunist threat to the life of Sir Edward or his wife, and are similarly inclined against kidnap. The deliberate targeting of the study and information that has reached us from our intelligence division leads us to suspect that German spies, or pro-German elements, mounted this operation as a fact-finding mission to discover the links that Sir Edward has to the British

Government. It is not ... unlikely that the German secret services were involved directly. Chief Inspector Carlisle and his men are currently at work in London checking the foreign register, the Government records apparatus and the records of entry at ports to further the enquiry. Despite our current belief that there is no direct threat to Sir Edward and his wife, however, as I have just indicated a guard will be mounted on this house until further notice. Chief Inspector Carlisle has authorised it."

"Very well. I shall not hinder you with my own small inquiries. One final point ... how do you reconcile the precise nature of this crime as measured against the apparently random violence, which, I understand, accompanied the violation of Sir Edward's property in Belgravia?"

"I have had the full facts from my Scotland Yard counterpart, Inspector Terry, leading the London end of the investigation only this afternoon. Sir Edward conducts much of his business from his Belgravia property and hence has more extensive and perhaps more sensitive papers at that property than here. Like here, the study was compromised when the locks were forced. Unlike here, the study was left in a state of shambolic disarray. Every paper and document seems to have been turned over. Mind you, the same was true of the entire house; it had been utterly ransacked. When considering the removal of the silver and artwork from the property, it is tempting to conclude that the offence was one of simple theft, carried out by thieves intent on making some easy money in the destructive manner so typical of these despicable people. But there is clearly more to it than that. The co-incidence of timing with the events here, for one thing. And while items were indeed removed from Belgravia, I believe that this was no more than a blind, a sideshow, designed to divert attention away from the intruders' real reason for being in the house, namely, Sir Edward's files. While I said just now that the house was ransacked, a lot of attention was paid to the contents of the study, and it is the considered opinion of Inspector Terry in Belgravia that the methods used in the property indicate an efficient and brutal search pattern."

"Hmm. Well, well, we shall see what tomorrow will bring."

It was now late so Hawkins showed us to our quarters in the west wing of the house, where the bulk of the accommodation was situated. The stark reality of our situation was brought home to us by the presence of a plainclothes man sitting in a chair on the landing off which Sir Edward and Lady Muster had their bedroom. Although Holmes had been non-committal during our conversation with Inspector Jackson I remembered from the past how that investigative mind would be working, analysing the facts and building up a case profile. As usual, I tried to put myself in his shoes and use his methods. As usual, I found I could not advance myself beyond the conclusions offered by Inspector Jackson. I turned in with a feeling of curiosity as to what the next day might bring.

Chapter Three

Mr Sherlock Holmes Investigates

At eight o'clock the following morning I descended the stairs to breakfast in the long hall to find Holmes already busy at work on bacon and eggs, the morning papers leaning against his coffee pot. Apart from the maid serving us the place was deserted, with Holmes explaining that Sir Edward was overseeing the fitting of new French windows in his study, while Jackson had caught an early train to London to confer with colleagues.

"Ah, Watson!" he cried. "You may be amused to see that the national newspapers clearly have the same taste for sensationalism as you yourself have exhibited in your chronicles of our adventures together." He held up *The Times* and *The Daily Mail.* 'Legendary Detective to assist prominent Anglophile' said the former; 'Sherlock Holmes: Bodyguard to German financier' cried the latter.

"The second is the most trite," grimaced Holmes, as he buttered some toast. "I would also be interested to know how the press discovered I was engaged on this case so quickly. I know Mycroft did not leak the information."

"There must have been local reporters here yesterday, Holmes. Perhaps one of the detectives or household let slip your forthcoming involvement."

"Perhaps," said Holmes doubtfully. "In any case there is work to be done, Watson. I shall start in the gardens whence the two nighthawks made their escape. This afternoon I shall interview the staff. This evening Sir Edward has graciously included us on his list of dinner guests for the event that friend Jackson referred to last night. Our course of action may, I think, be clearer at the conclusion of all these proceedings."

Sea Marge gardens were seventy-five yards wide and stretched for approximately one hundred yards from the patio behind the house down to the cliff edge, which in turn dropped steeply seventy feet to the sand and pebble beach. As I have mentioned, the patio and gardens were adorned with Romanesque statues and the lawn was heavily interspersed with bushes and herbaceous plants; many of these clumps were easily big enough for a man to hide behind. On each side with the exception of the cliff side the gardens were bordered with brick walls that ran from the very edge of the cliff all the way up to the house. These were of no less than fifteen feet in height, topped with vicious-looking metal spikes of a further two feet in height.

Holmes and I walked round the gardens in their entirety and then stood in the centre of the back gardens and looked up at the house. Seagulls cawed above us and the air was fresh with the smell of the sea.

"I can see why our intruders came at the house from the back," mused Holmes. "If the study was indeed their ultimate target, as seems logical, the French windows open directly onto the back patio. Moreover, with the exception of the heavily locked and bolted oak doors built into the house on each side of the property there is no thoroughfare between the front lawn and the back gardens. Let us also not forget that, as we saw last night, the front of the property is well illuminated at night thus making an unseen approach that much more difficult, whereas the rear of the house is shrouded in darkness. The question now is, did they come over the side walls, which on the face of the matter would seem to be the more likely option given their apparent skill in covert entry techniques, or did they approach from the beach?"

"The latter hypothesis is far from proven. The use of a small boat to gain access to the foot of the cliffs would seem to be ... unlikely given the inclement weather of the evening in question, and, as Bishop informed us last night, the waters off this coast are not to be underestimated. In addition the maid who served us at breakfast informed me before your arrival that the beach below this cliff is cut off at high tide. I consulted a booklet from Sir Edward's library before we came out here this morning that informed me that high tide on Friday night was at five minutes to midnight. If we consider the timing, if our nighthawks had approached from the beach a boat would have been necessary as the tide would have prevented avenues of approach and escape along the shore."

"What if the men had got into position earlier Holmes, and had been surveying Sir Edward's study for some time prior to the break-in? If they had moved into position earlier in the day a boat would not have been required as the tide would have been further out."

Holmes nodded approvingly. "Good, Watson! To take this theory further, it was only the untimely interruption of Wilson that caused the men to flee; it may have been that they intended to spend more time on the property, engage in a thorough search, and then make good their escape along the beach after the tide was well turned, at perhaps three or four o'clock in the morning. This is a distinct possibility, Watson.

Bishop told me that Sir Edward employs two gardeners who were at work in the gardens yesterday afternoon, until nightfall at half past five. Whilst a surveillance party would have risked discovery from these gardeners in daylight hours, there is a definite window of opportunity for our intruders to take up position any time after six o'clock. These intruders were professionals. They seem, somehow, to have known the routines of Sir Edward, his family and his staff and would have planned accordingly. They knew the layout of the house, as least as far as the location of and entrance to the study was concerned. They would have hoped for a clear run at the building once Sir Edward had retired to bed. And, while these men had not planned on being interrupted, it is just possible that the tide had retreated sufficiently by half past one this morning to expose sufficient sand for a desperate escape on foot back along the beach."

"How would these people have overcome the problem posed by operating in the dark with no clear source of illumination?" I asked. "The low cloud cover engendered by the storm would, I imagine, have obscured any moonlight that might have been available."

"I know that specialist oil lamps are available for use in hazardous conditions," replied my friend, "robustly designed so as to afford the user visibility but at the same time protecting the internal workings from inclement weather conditions, hard knocks, and so on. The problems posed by the dark environment could be overcome by the judicious utilisation of such devices. If, additionally, the intruders were familiar with this immediate area and stretch of coast, then the problems associated with night-time infiltration would automatically be lessened."

Holmes paused, and then continued.

"Whilst there may still be issues with our nautical theory, to me it presents a more compelling possibility than that of our intruders entering these grounds over the walls. You noted yourself in our stroll just now what a formidable physical barrier these walls comprise. Aside from the towering brickwork an intruder would have to deal with the lethal spikes atop the wall, a severe hazard. To negotiate such an obstacle, while not utterly impossible perhaps, would undoubtedly take particular equipment and, more importantly, time. Mycroft told me, and this was confirmed by Jackson last night, that within a minute of the alarm being raised Sir Edward's entire household, nine people in all, were in the gardens hunting for the intruders. My assessment is that these men would have been very pushed for time to effect an escape over such a formidable barrier in such a short and pressed period of time, and Wilson's testimony seems to indicate they were heading downhill towards the beach. Jackson himself still favours the idea that they came over the wall. He cannot entertain the possibility that in the dark and adverse weather an attempt was made from the seaward side. Yet even he admits that he had twenty policemen from the Norfolk force comb these gardens yesterday, and the other sides of the walls, and they came across nothing that indicated entry or exit over the walls; no trace of ladder indentation marks, or rope, no crushed bush or footprint in the mud, no tear of cloth."

"So, to follow for the moment the idea that the two men escaped via the beach, let us take ourselves down to the cliff face."

Standing looking back at the house from the cliff face Holmes continued to expound the theory he favoured. "You can see Watson, that the varying shrubs, small trees and statues present in increasing quantities as one reaches the farthest reaches of the gardens would provide an excellent cover for two people running for the cliff. And turning our attention to the seaward side, although this is a relatively steep drop, you can clearly see that Sir Edward has thoughtfully installed a set of wooden steps for easy access to the shore. This is the obvious place for our men to make for. Even though Jackson's men searched this area and found nothing, I feel it may repay us to cover this ground at the top of the cliff and steps again. I only hope that anything of value has not already been obliterated by the feet of so many heavy-heeled representatives of the local constabulary," he added grimly.

The wooden steps proved too weather-beaten and bare to yield any clues, but after an hour and a half's perusal of the site, Holmes gave a cry.

"I was right, Watson, our fugitives did pass this way." Holmes stooped to a small patch of mud near a gorse bush at the top of the steps and indicated what could only be part of a footprint, a round whorl and meandering lines indicating what seemed to belong to a soft shoe.

"A plimsoll, Watson, or I miss my guess," said Holmes, studying his find intently through his ubiquitous magnifying glass. "Jackson's men must have missed it. Our men were fleet of foot and, given the proclivity for this type of footwear among our seagoing folk, the probability is that they were maritime or naval sorts. The very fact they headed for the cliff and the sea on such a night reinforces the fact that they were salty adventurers. This seems a reasonable conclusion to draw irrespective of whether a small boat featured in their operation or not."

Holmes looked down on to the beach below where two or three crab boats and a steam powered fishing smack were drawn up very high on the beach. Then he smiled. "It appears we progress, Watson. A skilful break-in is carried out by men of some nautical background." The smile faded. "It is to be hoped that they did not drown as a result of their actions ..."

"Will you advise Jackson?" I queried.

"Presently perhaps. But you will remember that I am an independent investigator. Before I submit my report to Mycroft I may well share any snippets with the good Inspector if I feel it will advance his solving of the case. Come, let us return to the house for some refreshment."

Before we entered the house by the French windows of the study Holmes spent a period of time scanning the patio. Finally he gave a cry and knelt down.

"Look, Watson. This is where our men stood, just prior to forcing Sir Edward's study, I would venture." Not far from the study doors, under cover of the veranda, Holmes pointed to some dried sand, and what looked like the faintest traces of cigarette ash. "This is where the men left the last of their sand from the beach after their approach to the house." Holmes used a penknife to carefully scoop up the cigarette ash, and sniffed it. "*Players Navy Cut*, Watson, or I don't know my tobacco." He looked up at me and smiled. "Beloved by sailors and fishermen all over the country. This case is leading into interesting waters. Not a word to the others, yet, mind!"

"What of Jackson's idea that this was a German operation?" I asked.

For reply my friend just shrugged and smiled. "It is early days, yet, Watson." He tapped his nose and we passed indoors to enjoy coffee and a luncheon.

41

The afternoon was spent interviewing the members of Sir Edward's household in one of the withdrawing rooms in the lower west wing of the house. These comprised Sir Edward himself; Lady Stefanie; Bishop the driver; Hawkins the butler; Wilson, Sir Edward's private secretary and general manager; four catering and waiting staff, and the two gardeners that Sir Edward employed on a part-time basis. Holmes conducted the interviews in a pleasant but astute way, and it soon became apparent that the total ignorance of all parties with regards to maritime and nautical matters made it difficult to associate any one of them with the activities of the resourceful intruders of the evening in question. Similarly I could tell that Holmes was probing for any evidence of a possible blackmail motive or opportunity among the members of Sir Edward's staff, but as I suspected at the time, and as Holmes later confirmed, he could not in all honesty label any of his interviewees a potential blackmailer on the results of his conversations. All the staff gave the impression of loyalty to the Muster family and could add very little to the enquiry above that which had already been revealed to us. Moreover, all the domestic staff, both in Norfolk and in London, had been with their employer some time and there had been no recent recruits whose loyalty could be considered suspect.

Lady Stefanie Muster answered all Holmes' questions formally and I could sense that despite her reserve of the previous night, the experience had frightened her badly. She and Sir Edward had met at a social evening in London and had been happily married for the past nine years, but owing to their coming together fairly late in life (she was forty-seven when they met and he forty-four) did not have any children. I understood that the family assets would revert to the Muster dynasty on their departing this world. "Edward and I have been exceptionally happy together," she smiled. "I have no regrets at having no family of our own. However, I do admit that this recent business has caused me some consternation."

Holmes, demonstrating the kindliness in his nature that he seldom revealed, patted her arm. "I give you my word that Watson and I will not rest until this unpleasant affair is cleared up," he smiled.

Wilson, Sir Edward's business manager, proved himself fiercely protective of his employer's business affairs and interests, and adopted a slightly belligerent attitude under Holmes' questioning. But again, his loyalty to Sir Edward seemed absolute. We gathered that he acted as Sir Edward's personal aide and had ultimate responsibility for the overall running of Sir Edward's British interests. This included overseeing his travel plans and often accompanying his employer when Sir Edward went abroad, as well as managing his political dealings. We were advised that Sir Edward had not been involved directly in anything of a political nature for the past six months; we understood this to mean that he had not engaged in activities or discussions with members of the British or German Governments on any issue relating to domestic or foreign policy, and that he had only been abroad once in that time period, to Holland and thence Germany respectively, in January.

"To what end, pray?" asked Holmes.

"A business conference in Holland, followed by some banking business in Frankfurt," advised Mr Wilson, in a curious singsong voice.

Wilson seemed curiously evasive about this trip abroad, even as Holmes' questioning became more direct.

"Does it not appear curious to you, Mr Wilson, that the assaults on the properties of Sir Edward take place now, when each are teeming with staff and owners, whereas the same operations could have been mounted in January against reduced households with a consequently reduced risk of discovery? Do you not stop to consider that something your employer discovered, or brought back with him from Europe this time, may have prompted these raids?"

Wilson shrugged, but maintained his guarded air. "I am maintaining Sir Edward's personal and commercial confidence. If Sir Edward chooses to share more information with you about these recent excursions, that is his business, but I shall say no more."

Holmes sighed and spread his hands to indicate that the interview had ended.

Finally we spoke to Sir Edward. Holmes immediately raised the issue of his mysterious trip to the continent in January, which had been alluded to by both Bishop and Wilson.

"Sir Edward, it would help me greatly to know the circumstances of your visits to Holland and Germany last month."

"I would prefer ... not to discuss the matter, if I may," said Sir Edward with a fixed smile. "I can assure you that these visits were purely of a business nature. I cannot believe that they can have any relevance to the case in hand."

"As you wish," replied Holmes. "I am an independent observer and have no official status. But I should be frank with you, Sir Edward, that in all my previous cases I have always obtained the best results when my clients have been candid and honest with me, and left it to me to judge what is, or is not, important."

I could see that Muster's naturally good and honest nature was at odds with laying this obstruction in front of Holmes. There was silence for a few moments.

"I was at a business conference in The Hague for two weeks in January," he said at last. "After that I went to Frankfurt briefly to address some business concerns I had with my German banking interests. The conference and its results could have adversely affected some of my key business interests, and its ramifications are ongoing, which is why I find the matter sensitive and am reluctant to air it in open forum, even with you, Mr Holmes."

"Thank you," said Holmes. "Let us leave it at that for now. But may we proceed on the assumption that if I require further clarification on any aspect of these visits you will render it to me instantly?"

"Of course," said Muster, "if you feel it to be necessary as your study of the case advances, then it is agreed." The moment of awkwardness passed. Sir Edward was far more forthcoming in other details of his personal and business career and we spent an informative half hour on these matters.

"What are your immediate plans for inspecting the damage to your London property, and assessing the losses, Sir Edward?" asked Holmes.

Sir Edward snorted. "The police want me to stay here under close protection for at least the next few days," he said in disgust. "This is not how I would like to play it. Whoever these intruders were, if I alter my routine and give the impression that my life has been affected, it is playing into their hands. Moreover, I am very anxious, as you say, to inspect my London home. The only saving grace, which prevents me from lobbying forcefully to be allowed back to town immediately, is that my man in Belgravia, Barker, has compiled a full inventory of items stolen and damage incurred to the property which I am sure will be accurate to the letter. I have also spoken with him at length on the incursion into my study and it seems as if my papers, though violated, are complete and intact."

"You place considerable faith in this ... Barker?" queried Holmes.

"The sole of reliability, organisational excellence, and discretion. He has been with me since I arrived here in the 1890s. Barker's report and findings will be accurate, I am sure."

Holmes took up his propelling pencil and made a brief comment in his notebook. "Would you be so good as to supply me with your Belgravia address, Sir Edward?"

"Number Four, Halkin Place, SW1. Do you intend to go down there?"

Holmes smiled. "I have a wide-ranging investigative brief, Sir Edward, and am not constrained by policy or police directives. It may well be that at some point I will need to visit Halkin Place. May I ask two favours of you?"

"Of course," replied the knight, puzzled.

"I will need a letter, written and signed by yourself, giving me your authority to inspect your London home, that I can present to Barker when I see fit. The second favour that I ask is that you tell no one in your household, not even Detective Inspector Jackson or his Special Branch associates my movements or anything I choose to confide in you until I advise you otherwise. Is that understood?"

"Of course," said Sir Edward, looking mystified. "But why a handwritten letter? I can ask Wilson to send a telegram tomorrow."

Holmes flashed his most winning smile. "A handwritten note would be better … for now. I prefer to keep my enquiries and movements as hidden as possible until I judge the moment right to reveal them. It is an old habit to which I adhere, and one that has served me well. Remember, do not disclose anything of my movements to anyone. Let Watson handle questions pertaining to my work and whereabouts."

"As you say. I just need to visit my study." Sir Edward went off to his study and a few minutes later returned with an envelope, which he handed to Holmes. "That instructs all my household staff, and, if you have cause to visit my offices in London, all my business staff, to assist you in any way you see fit. My business card is enclosed in there with details of my office address in High Holborn."

"If your group of companies have recruited any new staff to your offices at High Holborn recently, I presume full details will be kept on file. May I be permitted to view them?" asked Holmes.

"Certainly," replied Sir Edward. "That letter of authority allows you to do anything like that."

"How are you managing your business affairs at present, Sir Edward," I ventured, "given the current restrictions on your movements?"

"As it happens I was nearing the end of a two-week holiday up here at Sea Marge when this unpleasantness occurred. I was resting following the visit abroad before returning to work in London. In the event Wilson has been managing my business affairs for me by telephone, telegram and post, and will continue to do so until I am given leave to return to town. In future I hope to spend more and more time here so it is a business arrangement I hope will succeed on a practical level."

Holmes rose and shook Sir Edward's hand. "And now," he went on, consulting his pocket watch, "it is already half past five and high time that I changed for dinner. It is very good of you to include us on your dinner invitation at such late notice, Sir Edward, and I must confess that it is seldom that I dine in such esteemed company as promises to be the case tonight."

Seven o'clock saw Holmes and myself, smartly attired in dinner suits, sipping dry sherry with Sir Edward in the long dining room in the centre of Sea Marge. This magnificent room sported a splendid oak dining table and was likewise panelled entirely in oak, with hunting scenes carved into the woodwork. The Special Branch men had attempted to be as unobtrusive as possible but their number patrolling the house and grounds had now been increased to ten; no doubt the guest list for the evening had ensured these increased precautions. Prior to the aperitif with Sir Edward, Holmes had stolen a quick word with Inspector Jackson who had returned from London after conferring with his opposite number on the Belgravia case. He brought with him his superior, Chief Inspector Carlisle, a tall heavily built man with the unmistakeable air of command and authority that sometimes comes with men of rank, and five more men from the Special Branch reserve; hard-looking men who, in their outlook and bearing, seemed to me to bear the stamp of former military personnel. I gathered from Holmes that little direct progress had been made in the case, although attempts were ongoing in London to identify foreign nationals whom the police believed may be of interest to the enquiry.

Esteemed guests soon began to arrive at Sea Marge and by half past seven a convivial gathering had formed in the long dining room. Aside from Sir Edward and Lady Muster, Holmes and myself, those present included the retired banker

Lord Hillingdon with his wife, Lady Beatrice, the property magnate Lord Battersea who came alone as his wife Marjorie was unwell, the retired iron merchant Sir Daniel Everard, and the retired civil servant Max Moorhouse, late of the Home Office. I gathered that First Lord of the Admiralty Winston Churchill, and his wife, Clementine, had been due to attend but had been unavoidably detained in London at the eleventh hour.

Finding myself seated next to a gregarious local businessman, Michael Benbow, at dinner, I was soon deep in discussion on local issues as I attacked a most excellent roast Norfolk pheasant with all the trimmings. The Churchills, I learnt, retained Pear Tree Cottage, two minutes walk from Sea Marge, all the year round and often spent Christmas there, although naturally enough it was more favoured as a summer retreat. I questioned him on Bishop's comment of the previous evening that, since he had been made First Sea Lord the previous October he liked to travel up to Norfolk on the Admiralty yacht or perhaps by Royal Navy warship, so that he, his family and servants could be ferried ashore to Overstrand beach by local boats. Benbow confirmed this was so, and I found myself chuckling inwardly at the First Sea Lord commanding government resources to effect his frequent trips to the coast.

As main course gave way to dessert and coffee I discoursed with my other neighbour, Max Moorhouse, the retired civil servant, who seemed amused to learn that the authorities thought the attacks on Sir Edwards' properties were so serious as to warrant the involvement of the great Sherlock Holmes over and above that of the Metropolitan Police Service. I told him what I knew – that Mycroft had engaged his brother as an independent investigator due to his personal association with Sir Edward and also because of the unique position of Sir Edward with regards to Anglo-German relations. I learnt little of Moorhouse's own career; he seemed evasive when I asked him what his involvement had been with the Home Office, merely saying that he had been heavily involved in policy and research, and seemed more interested in hearing tales of my adventures with Holmes before the turn of the century. I did, however, gather that he had retired to Cromer a few years ago just after his wife passed away.

The same was broadly true of Sir Daniel Everard, the retired steel merchant, who had moved to Overstrand from London in 1910 following the sudden death of his wife, leaving the family firm in the controlling hands of his two sons. He himself did not look in good health. A short, rotund man with a round, bespectacled face, he was overweight and his features showed signs of years of good living. Despite a pasty white complexion, whenever I looked over at him that evening I could discern a sheen of perspiration which glistened on his brow. Several times I noticed him deep in discussion with Sherlock Holmes. I personally did not get an opportunity to speak to Sir Daniel that evening, with the exception of the introductory pleasantries, and as the party left the dinner table and retired into the withdrawing room for brandy and cigars I fell into conversation with Lady Beatrice Hillingdon, who enthused about the Norfolk countryside and the benefits of the Cromer air on the constitution. I was still in conversation on the merits of retaining a property in North Norfolk with Lords Hillingdon and Battersea when the evening began to draw to a close. Guests began to leave just after midnight and by a quarter to one there was merely Holmes, Sir Edward and myself left in the withdrawing room. Sir Edward had dismissed the servants for the night and Lady Muster had also turned in.

After a brief nightcap Sir Edward rose and bade us goodnight. A few moments after he had left Holmes also rose.

"Join me in my rooms for a moment before you turn in, old friend. I have some instructions for the 'morrow."

Seated in the anteroom of my friend's quarters, Holmes launched into a series of instructions for the coming day.

"Watson, I require you to make some enquiries as to the nature of the shore and tides along this stretch of coast, and also of the type of boat which our two nighthawks may have employed to effect entry to, and escape from, these grounds the other evening. Spend some time in the local library, speak to the local fishermen, pick up any details you can of unusual events, unusual persons being seen in the vicinity – seafaring types other than the honest local fishermen, for example, any items of gossip you may come across."

"A wide-ranging brief," I sniffed.

My colleague continued as if he had not heard me. "I also require you, in case of my absence, to keep fully informed as to the progress of the investigation as carried out by Inspector Jackson, Chief Inspector Carlisle, and their associates."

"You can rely on me, Holmes. I shall do my very best. But where will you be?"

Holmes rose and went over to the window, twitching aside the curtain to reveal a drizzling rain illuminated by the lamps on the outside of the property.

"I may still be here in Overstrand. Then again, I may not. I shall probably have to go to London at some juncture over the next day or two, to cast my eye over the business in Belgravia. But turning to matters of more immediate interest, tell me,

Watson, what did you think of our fellow dinner guests of this evening?"

Slightly thrown by this change of tack, I went on to give a measured evaluation of those with whom I had spoken at length. "Sir Daniel Everard," I concluded, "I did not really speak to, but I would venture that as a medical man he looked to me as if he was suffering from some illness, possibly caused or exacerbated by an unhealthy lifestyle in the past."

"Ah," said Holmes turning, "I spoke at length with Sir Daniel on a number of topics, including his past career and the present fortunes of the family firm he built up. He told me he has a house in Back Lane in Overstrand, not five minutes walk from here and overlooking the sea. There were other aspects of our conversation that were more revealing. He admitted to a penchant for collecting antique weapons. He also professed to be a lover of art and fine tobacco, so I, with my small knowledge of these subjects, endeavoured to steer the conversation round to these topics. Time after time he stumbled and made elementary mistakes in response to my questions that led me to deduce that he was indeed fond of art and tobacco, but that he was otherwise mentally preoccupied to such a degree that it was impairing his knowledge and the quality of his conversation. He was drinking exceptionally heavily. It became clear to me that this man's nerves are in shreds, and a nervous collapse of some description seems a real possibility. You ask me, Watson, what I am doing tomorrow. The answer is that for the immediate future I am going to concern myself with the activities of Sir Daniel Everard. As I intimated to Sir Edward earlier, if anyone asks as to my whereabouts do pretend innocence; deflect the enquiry and say that you are used to me working alone and keeping you in the dark."

"The immediate threat against Sir Edward's interests is past, and there are now a number of armed policemen protecting his wellbeing and that of his household. You have kindly agreed to pursue the nautical evidence that we uncovered this morning. Personally, as I have a roving brief here in Overstrand, I have no hesitation in shadowing Sir Daniel and pursuing this line of enquiry to see where it may lead."

"You do not think that Sir Daniel's nervous state is a purely medical problem?" I enquired.

"Oh he is clearly in poor health, Watson, there is no disputing it. But there is something more. That man is scared, Watson. Terribly scared." He turned away thoughtfully.

Chapter Four

Mr Sherlock Holmes Discourses

The following day I undertook the duties that Holmes had laid upon me manfully, and walked down into Cromer after an early breakfast to research the matters he had entrusted me with. I say I had an early breakfast, and yet there was no sign of Holmes, who I gathered from the maid had not attended breakfast at all. My first avenue of enquiry led me to speak to a number of fishermen who were repairing pots and nets among a cluster of crab boats drawn up on Cromer beach. Initially reserved, they warmed to me when they heard I was a companion of the great Sherlock Holmes. From them I gathered that the crab boat, a small shallow-bottomed craft, was the most common *mode d'emploi* of the fisherfolk along these shores owing to its manoeuvrability and suitability for inshore waters where sandbanks threatened. I reached the conclusion that such a boat could have negotiated the foot of Overstrand cliffs on the night in question if manned by competent sailors, but the weather and the dark would have made the operation intensely difficult.

I was of the belief that strangers, or unfamiliar persons, would stand out in such an environment of 'locals' as Overstrand and Cromer but clearly this was not the case. I learnt that fishermen and sailors from all over the United Kingdom and Europe put into the ports along this stretch of coast, so there was nothing unusual in seeing unfamiliar faces. The excellent herring harvests were exacerbating this situation as more boats and more people were in the area than may otherwise have been the case. Add to this situation the influx of holidaymakers into Cromer during certain times of the year and the town became a veritable melting-pot of humanity. I gathered during my conversations that the headline news as far as the local fishing community was concerned was the surprise loss of two fishing boats, one just along the coast and another in Dutch waters, both of which had occurred about a week previously. Later, in the Cromer library, I read the newspaper reports of these events and noted the names of these vessels and a few pertinent details. I also read widely on the local economy and strengthened my knowledge of the herring harvest, which appeared to be reaping great profits for those presently engaged in it. I also researched the nature of the local sea and weather conditions. In the afternoon I headed back to Overstrand, confident that I had the wherewithal to submit a competent report to my friend, particularly on the likelihood and nature of a seaborne infiltration of Sir Edward's property the other evening.

I spent the remainder of the afternoon at Sea Marge, observing the activities of the Special Branch officers who were still patrolling the property and residing at temporary lodgings locally when off duty. The new arrival, Carlisle, and several of his subordinates seemed to be spending a great deal of time in Sir Edward's study, although what else they hoped to learn after this advanced passage of time baffled me. Similarly, his other men appeared to be active throughout the property and indeed throughout the village, as I espied one of them outside the Post Office during an afternoon preamble through the village.

At just before six o'clock in the evening I took a telephone call from Mr Sherlock Holmes in Sir Edward's study. Holmes was in London. All my bewildered questions as to his whereabouts and activities were batted away by my friend, who merely advised that he had 'made progress' and was seeking my permission to stay for the night at my rooms in Queen Anne Street. Of course I acquiesced. However, just as I was preparing to regale my friend with the results of my wide-ranging research, he rang off as if in a fearful hurry and left me grasping a silent receiver.

The following day was spent again observing the curious activities of the Special Branch men, who roamed throughout Sea Marge and kept a vigil in front of and behind the house. They appeared interested in every aspect of the property, and I saw them inspecting every feature imaginable from the doors and windows to a small balcony, high up in the middle of the property on the second floor, which faced seaward. I enquired of the new arrival, Chief Inspector Carlisle, what possible interest his men could have in such a minute coverage of Sea Marge, and was curtly advised that they were sounding out the property to discover the security weaknesses of the building in order to advise Sir Edward accordingly. The brusque and overbearing Mr Carlisle seemed a very different proposition to the friendly and earnest Inspector Jackson. I noticed that Jackson was less in evidence at Sea Marge following the arrival of his superior, and it appeared that responsibility for the house now devolved largely upon Carlisle and the detail of men recently arrived from London.

Later on in the day I chatted with a few fishermen at the bottom of Overstrand cliffs, who reinforced the impressions I had received from their Cromer counterparts the previous day. I took tea with my new friend Benbow at his cottage in Overstrand, spending a pleasing hour chatting over local gossip and information. I also saw Sir Edward, who was chafing to have this business behind him, complaining loudly about being interviewed by Special Branch again and stating impatiently that he wanted to 'get on'.

It was half past ten in the evening when Mr Sherlock Holmes returned to Overstrand, and I spent the first twenty minutes watching him wolf down a cold supper. After this we again adjourned to the anteroom of his quarters, presumably to ensure that our ensuing discussions would not be overheard.

"Well now, Watson," he began, smoke rising from his pipe. His face was serious. "It has been a most illuminating ... and worrying ... thirty-six hours. Whatever it is we have stumbled upon here, the roots of the affair run deep. I believe this business at Sir Edward's is merely the tip of a dark and sinister iceberg. First you shall tell me how you have got on, and then I shall tell you how I have got on."

With this cryptic statement hanging in the air, I gave Holmes a detailed evaluation of my discoveries over the preceding period. In truth I was unsure as to the benefit of my own small enquiries with regard to the resolution of this business, but to my surprise Holmes listened intently to all I told him, without the usual brash interference or contradictions that so often accompanied my reports to him.

When I concluded, he stared at the ceiling in silent contemplation for a good few minutes.

"Thank you," he said.

"And now what of you, and what on earth took you to London," I asked, incredulously.

Holmes looked at me, and then launched into his own remarkable tale.

"You will remember that as the evening before last drew to a close I announced to you my intention of keeping a very close eye on the activities of Sir Daniel Everard. I must confess that my little plan bore fruit in ways that were as dramatic and unexpected as they were immediate. Before breakfast yesterday, as it was becoming light, I left Sea Marge with the intention of taking a walk around the village and, specifically, reconnoitring the area around Back Lane where Sir Daniel resides. Back Lane is the last road in the village before the settlement gives way to countryside and pastureland once more, so it was fairly easy for me to get my bearings and mount a swift reconnaissance. Sure enough, I pinpointed Sir Daniel's pleasant property, The Gables, at the end of the lane with views to seaward. As it was still early I took myself up on to the ridge above Overstrand to better sample the fresh morning sea air, intending to return to the property and intercept the housemaid, Sir Daniel's only employed member of staff, as she arrived at work at half past eight. Sir Daniel had mentioned to me at dinner the previous evening that he employed a housemaid but I had been unable to elicit a name or address. My hope was that she would grant a private interview with me and cast further light on whatever fears and illness were undermining her employer."

"As I descended from the ridge, however, and with The Gables in sight I saw Sir Daniel Everard, wearing heavy overcoat and scarf as if dressed for a lengthy period out of doors, pull shut the latched gate in his front garden and hurry up Back Lane in the direction of the village proper. The furtive way in which he carried himself and glanced around as he moved up the road ... he did not see me ... intrigued me and I determined to follow him; if spotted I could always explain away my activity with the harmless explanation of a daily constitutional. Sir Daniel proceeded the two miles into Cromer town centre and, shortly after nine o'clock, entered Cromer Post Office, where he remained for several minutes, and thereupon left in a considerable hurry in the direction of Cromer Beach railway station."

"From my vantage point in a shop across the street I could see he was clearly agitated, perspiring heavily and strained of expression. I slipped into the Post Office after he had left and asked of the clerk what business Sir Daniel had conducted just moments before. Thankfully my past reputation secured his complete cooperation and he allowed me a look at the text of a telegram Sir Daniel had only recently dictated, destined for a Post Office box in London, for the attention of a person named Frederick Mountfield. The text of the missive was trite ... a request to see his old friend in Norfolk once again with the comment that the chess board awaited ... and the joviality of the correspondence could not, to my mind, be reconciled with the highly strung and fearful state of the individual who had vacated the Post Office only moments earlier. Clearly a code, or cover of some description, was being employed, and I resolved to follow Sir Daniel to see where my trail might lead. I made a rapid note of the Post Office box number and the call sign of the receiving Post Office in London, and headed down towards the station after Sir Daniel. There was a chance I would have lost my quarry, or even that the railway station was not his ultimate destination, but I was in luck and I espied him on the London platform among a knot of other travellers."

I sat absorbed as my friend continued.

"Keeping a low profile, I observed Sir Daniel pacing the platform, evidently awaiting the half past nine departure to Norwich and London. Thankfully the press of other travellers ensured he did not see me. The train arrived moments later and, giving Sir Daniel time to board, I leapt aboard a rear carriage with but seconds to spare before the conductor blew his whistle and we departed. At Norwich I scanned the platform as we arrived and Sir Daniel was not in evidence among those who departed. The train carried on to London and sure enough, as I disembarked at Liverpool Street, I caught sight of Sir Daniel hurrying into the crowds thronging the arrivals hall. I managed to keep him under surveillance as he moved away from the station and headed towards the East End of London, moving hurriedly down the Bethnal Green Road."

"The human traffic on the street had changed from city pinstripe to barrow boys, street vendors and market-sellers of all types and descriptions by the time my quarry crossed the road and entered a small tobacconist store with the appellation 'Haag's Gentlemens Tobacconists' picked out in gold and black lettering on the window and above the entrance. Whatever else this establishment may have been, I do not believe it to have been a shop frequented by clientele matching this description. It struck me as unusual that Sir Daniel should make a trip to such a seemingly out-of-the-way and down-at-heel tobacconists, when due to his station in life and professed love and appreciation of tobacco, you may expect him to patronise the very best vendors of Piccadilly. I decided to watch and wait. From my position in a café across the street I could see Sir Daniel talking in an animated fashion with a short man dressed in a white shirt and waistcoat, who I took to be the proprietor. After a few minutes the short man came to the window, had a look around outside, and reversed the sign on his glass front door to read 'Closed'. Whereupon he and Sir Daniel disappeared into the back of the building via a door at the rear of the shop."

"What happened next?" I interjected.

"I waited for the best part of two hours and considered abandoning my quarry to make further enquiries regarding the tobacconists into which he had disappeared. As I was considering this option, however, the two men suddenly reappeared from the back of the shop with 'waistcoat' looking ready to resume business as usual, reversing the sign on his front door once more. Sir Daniel let himself out of the front door, hitched up his collar against a light wind, and began to retrace his steps back towards Liverpool Street station. I noticed that the proprietor watched him go as he crossed the road and until he was out of sight. It was immediately apparent to me, as I hurriedly paid my dues and left the café … forgetting my copy of *The Times* as I did so … that a change had been wrought in Sir Daniel during the previous two hours. Despite the muffler that protected his throat from the February chill, I could see enough of his face as he left to identify a change in his complexion to a ruddy red hue, a redness that could not altogether be explained by the chill in the air. In addition he walked in a decidedly erratic fashion and once or twice stumbled slightly as he negotiated the Bethnal Green Road. I am certain he was the worse for drink, Watson. I followed him as far as Liverpool Street once more and watched as he boarded the half past three service back to Cromer."

"You did not consider following him back to Norfolk?" I queried.

Holmes shook his head. "I was fairly convinced the purpose of his day's excursion was complete. He seemed to have a definite purpose in London and when that was accomplished he appeared to have no further aims for the day. I was reasonably certain he would return to Overstrand without interruption."

"What did you do next?"

"The day was wearing on but there were several other items I wished to pursue while I was in the Capital. As I was near the East End and wanted to discover all I could concerning Haag's Tobacconists and its mysterious proprietor, I determined to make contact once more with Wiggins and see if he still had contact with any of the bloodhounds who used to make up the Baker Street Irregulars. At the very least, I reasoned, he would in all probability possess the local knowledge I would require to discover the secrets behind number 554 Bethnal Green Road."

It will be recalled that The Baker Street Irregulars, led by the resourceful Wiggins, were a gang of street-urchins whom Holmes had cultivated during his heyday as a private investigator during the closing years of the nineteenth century. No other agency covered the metropolis in such a comprehensive fashion, as they moved swiftly and without creating suspicion among all social classes to be found in Victorian London, had an encyclopaedic knowledge of the city, and as eyes and ears on the street could not be bettered. Holmes had employed his Irregulars to good effect on more than one occasion, most famously in locating a missing steam vessel, the *Aurora*, in the case of *The Sign of Four*. Nevertheless, I was taken aback – The Baker Street Irregulars must all have passed their thirtieth year by now, and to my knowledge had scattered to the four winds even before Holmes had retired.

"My word Holmes," I replied, startled. "The Baker Street Irregulars have been disbanded for over twenty years. How did you attempt to contact them?"

"I have kept in touch with Wiggins over the years. I have not seen him for many a year but I knew he had worked hard to build up a wholesale fruit and vegetable business in the East End. I had his office address in Bethnal Green so I called upon him after I witnessed Sir Daniel's departure. He seemed pleased ... and surprised ... to see me but, after some pleasantries and reminiscing, promised to help with my enquiries. As I suspected, Watson, he has spent his business life as well as his deprived childhood in that area and knows it as well as any man could ... he promised to sound out contacts of his who may be able to shed some light on the shop and proprietor in question. I departed after having tea with him and he said he should have some information for me within twenty-four hours. I therefore agreed to interview him again at the same time the following day; that is, today. I put the closing minutes of yesterday afternoon to good use in consulting a Post Office directory and tracing the call sign of the receiving Post Office in the enigmatic telegram sent by Sir Daniel to a Mr Mountfield in London."

"Where was it, Holmes?"

"A busy Post Office near Oxford Circus. This would make sense if Mr Mountfield has reason to avoid drawing attention to himself ... the place is enormous and exceptionally busy at any time of day. The fact that Mr Mountfield clearly pays for a holding service for his telegrams, so he collects them at his convenience rather than being forced to disclose an address for delivery, suggests that he wishes to retain control and anonymity in the arrangement."

"Or he may be merely a travelling man, Holmes, possibly abroad frequently?"

"I concede that is a possibility. But most people tend to have telegrams forwarded on to them at their onward destination, is that not so, rather than setting up a *post restante* facility? These are, in my experience, not only expensive, but also rather rare. Let us also not forget that the telegram to Mountfield originated from the frankly puzzling behaviour of Sir Daniel Everard, which is in itself suspicious."

"Very Well. What else?"

"After this I spoke to you briefly and gained your permission to stay at your rooms in Queen Anne Street, for which my thanks."

"This morning I resolved to visit Sir Edward's home at Halkin Place in Belgravia, and also his offices in High Holborn, to ascertain as much as possible regarding the London end of the enquiry. I was in Belgravia, that famous sanctuary of the well-to-do, by nine o'clock this morning, and had no trouble in locating Sir Edward's place, a four storey town house with basement at the end of a mews. The Metropolitan Police were still on site as I arrived but their business was nearly concluded and they were preparing to leave. It was immediately apparent why the cracksmen involved in this operation had such an easy time of it; all the servants live in the basement, and a fire escape runs the length of the four storeys, giving access to a fire door on the way up and a hatch on the roof. I gathered from Inspector Terry in charge that the intruders had gained entrance to the

65

property via the hatch in the roof, and, as I say, with all the servants residing in the basement, these fellows had the run of the house without being discovered. I saw Barker, Sir Edward's man, who had got down to the business of repairing the damage and getting the household back on its feet very efficiently, and obtained from him a list of the few stolen goods, which really only covered a few pieces of silver and one or two works of art of a low value."

"Barker reiterated that all Sir Edward's paperwork had been recovered, but he stressed again the awful state in which the study was found. The lock on the study door in Halkin Place had been unceremoniously smashed, in a very different *modus operandi* to the delicate methods employed in Norfolk … I do concede, however, that it was a far more substantial lock than it's counterpart in Sea Marge. I am convinced, though, that papers or documentation were the reason for the raid. Barker advised me that all other areas capable of holding such material, such as a small writing bureau and a filing cabinet in Sir Edward's withdrawing room, had been methodically searched. Barker said that there were papers all over the place."

"Fundamentally I believe the same agency to have been behind both intrusions. I have yet to determine who or what that agency represents. Like Jackson, I am of the belief that the different *modus operandi* exhibited in Halkin Place, with its seemingly random violence and minor instances of common theft, was merely a clumsily executed attempt at a diversion designed to give rise to the idea that common thieves were behind the London offence, and were a separate group and pursuing a different agenda to the Norfolk nighthawks. Aside from the coincidence in timing, the theory of theft does not hold water for a further two reasons. First, if the motive of these individuals was to steal items of worth from Sir Edward, as one might expect common thieves to do, why did they not take more? Secondly, we can refute the idea of a theft to order as the items removed, even the artwork, would not have been of significant market value or rarity to have been worth the risk. Frankly, I would venture that the pieces in question would not interest a collector enough to commission the theft. As you know, Watson, I am something of an authority on art and I can tell you that the pieces stolen were unremarkable. Incidentally, I took the opportunity to interview the staff on site and came to the same conclusions regarding their collective integrity as I did with their equivalents here in Overstrand."

"What do the Metropolitan Police think of it?" I asked.

"Terry agreed with my assessment that documentation or information was the reason for the raid. He and Jackson pursue the theory that some German agency is responsible for both intrusions, and I kept my own counsel. From Belgravia I swiftly reconnoitred the Post Office near Oxford Circus I referred to earlier, then moved to the reading rooms of the British Library and elected, on my own initiative, to attempt to discover a little more surrounding the provenance of this mysterious conference that Sir Edward attended in The Hague last month. I reasoned that there was a strong possibility that his activities, those of a prominent international businessman, would be referenced in the *Financial Times* or the business sections of the other major dailies."

Here Holmes stood and listened briefly outside his door, as if to reassure himself that there was no possibility of us being overheard. Then he returned to his seat and took out his notebook.

He whistled softly. "My word, Watson, I can understand Sir Edward's reticence on the matter." He looked down at his notes. "Between December 1st last year and January 23rd of this, delegates from the major European powers, China, Japan and the United States of America gathered in The Hague in Holland for the American-sponsored International Opium Conference. The stated aims of the conference, as outlined by the Americans, were to immediately push for and agree binding international legislation that would ban the trade in opium as a commercial product. Very small quantities of items such as morphine and similar opium derivates, legitimately required for medicinal use, were to be exempt. The Americans seem to have been genuinely acting for humanitarian reasons, as opium addiction and misery in the Far East is well-publicised, but clearly such a policy, if approved, would have far-reaching implications for the British and the Dutch, particularly, who still realise considerable profits from the trade."

"The German delegation backed the proposal strongly, and reacted angrily against a British counter-proposal, probably introduced as a stalling measure, that cocaine also be covered by the terms of any agreed legislation with similar exemptions concerning legitimate medical use. The widespread and unfettered sale of cocaine is in turn a key component of the German economy. As we know Sir Edward himself has interests in pharmaceuticals, and it was he who, in the final two weeks of the conference, joined the German delegation and spoke powerfully and eloquently against the cocaine proposal. Eventually the conference broke up towards the end of January without achieving any of its aims, but the Americans have wrung a concession from all parties to reconvene again with a similar agenda next year. It appears,

Watson, that the exchanges between the British and German delegations became ever more heated and bitter, and can truly be said to have done further damage to an already brittle diplomatic relationship. The press in both countries covered the debates in ever more biased fashion. Sir Edward's role in the affair will have been marked. It is little wonder, as a man with a foot in both camps, so to speak, that he is so sensitive about his role in the proceedings. He could well have drawn unfavourable criticism on his return home to England. I am very much of the opinion that these raids on his premises are in some way related to the political repercussions of this conference."

"Now you mention it, Holmes, I seem to remember reading something about this conference in the newspapers. It did indeed seem a bitter affair. But you said just now that the conference broke up in acrimony on the 23rd of January. We know that Sir Edward was away in Frankfurt until the 1st of February ... so why wait until now to raid his houses?"

Holmes shook his head grimly. "I confess I do not know ... yet. But I will find out."

"Pray, continue," I intoned.

"From the British Library it is but a short hop to the High Holborn offices of Sir Edward. These redbrick buildings are smaller than I would have imagined, and consequently pay host to fewer staff. I swiftly interviewed the manager. He confirmed in answers to my questions that there had been no incidents of security violation there in the past two months; no reported break-ins, burglaries, thefts or the like, but that one new member of staff had been taken on recently. A messenger had been hired from early January ... the 11th was the hiring date ... but had left abruptly on 1st of February, without serving his week's notice. The gentleman in question had performed his duties well enough, but had kept himself to himself and my sources at Sir Edward's offices could tell me little about him. I did learn that he had been a bicycle courier delivering some of Sir Edward's business papers, however, and as such would have had limited access to the latter's private offices."

"In addition, I learnt that, in line with company policy, a photograph of each member of staff is kept along with their recruitment details. The *curriculum vitae* this gentleman, Mr Caulfield, had submitted did not quite seem to ring true; long periods of time spent abroad and hence largely unverifiable; but in his recruitment photograph I noticed several singular features. The face that glowered out at me from under a shock of straw-coloured hair was afflicted by a red birthmark affecting the right cheek. Clearly I could not identify colours from the photograph, but my contact confirmed them. Moreover, although the photograph of head and shoulders revealed few clothing details, he appeared to me to be sporting an outfit corresponding to a certain cut, such as a military uniform. One button of this uniform was just visible in the photograph, so, utilising the power of Sir Edward's letter to the full, I borrowed the photograph and took it to a photographic specialist I know on New Oxford Street to see whether he couldn't make a reproduction of the picture in a larger size. My plan was to see if I could identify the regimental crest and motto from the button, which in turn might leave an opening for further enquiries. Mr Radley will have a result for me by the end of tomorrow, so a return to town will be required at some juncture, depending on how the other lines of enquiry are progressing."

"My word, Holmes. You are uncovering and following a wide-ranging and disparate number of leads," I breathed.

"This afternoon was to bring the most sensational revelations to date. As I had arranged with Wiggins yesterday afternoon, I effected a *rendezvous* with him at half past three sharp at his offices in the East End. I was met by my young friend who was putting on his coat. 'Come with me, Mr Holmes,' he said to me. 'I've made a few enquiries and called in a few favours and I'm taking you to see Bob Gurney who works at the Post Office in Abernathy Street. He reckons he knows a bit about your Mr Haag'. As we left his offices on the short walk to the Post Office Wiggins kept up a running commentary. He had discovered that Haag was a second generation German immigrant whose family had moved to London from Germany in the 1850s. His father had been a watchmaker and surgical instrument maker. The family fortunes had been unimpressive, I gathered, but enough money had been left for their only son to set up a small business. Gunther Haag, I was advised, was a single man who lived above his shop."

"As we turned into Abernathy Street Wiggins knocked on an innocuous side door in the Post Office building and a small man with rat-like features ushered us surreptitiously inside. I found myself in what appeared to be a small sorting office, with large bins holding envelopes and packages of all shapes and sizes. Aside from our informant, the room was deserted. Wiggins quickly introduced me to his contact, a Mr Bob Gurney."

"My new informant eyed me craftily and spat on to the floor. He was chewing a large plug of tobacco, exposing a number of gaps in his blackened teeth. He looked to me like the sort of fellow who would like to be inside everyone's business ... whether bidden or not ... and I daresay, not slow to take advantage of any opportunity that might come his way as a result of that knowledge. Sure enough, this proved to be the case this afternoon. The gist of the conversation went along the following lines."

Holmes had always had a gift for, and delighted in, disguise and mimicry. He dropped into an East London accent as he impersonated the shifty Bob Gurney, and went on to recount parts of his conversation with the postal worker almost verbatim.

"'Gunther Haag is a German, Mr Holmes, and if I say so myself I know him better than most as I've delivered his mail for the last two years. He lives as quiet and modest a life as anyone I've ever come across and has courteous manners and is well-spoken to a fault. But something doesn't ring quite true. We have three deliveries of mail a day to deliver round here, Mr Holmes, and I can tell you that there are two things which have struck me as odd about our Mr Haag, him being merely a humble East End tobacco merchant and all. The first thing is that he has a quality of visitor that I find odd considering his position and calling in life. All hours of the day they seem to come, smart gentlemen in suits and fine wool coats and all, and they are not all going there for 'baccy', mark my words. I see these fine men disappear into the back of the shop with 'nary a look at the counter or his wares. And Gunther Haag, he does a good trade all right among the East End folk … people like him and he charges fair … but if he has no business when one of these fine fellows arrives, well, he just shuts up shop and accompanies his visitor to the rear of the shop and then, I guess, upstairs'."

"'The other strange thing is the amount of mail he receives, letters and parcels and the like. I can understand some deliveries to a small business like his, maybe some brochures and advertisements, and perhaps a few pieces of personal mail, but Haag receives far more than I would expect, the Lord knows. I reckon he is into black market goods meself. Mind you, they say the East End is like a big family and a community and nobody pries too much into anyone else's business, as long as it ain't harming no-one else. Also there's no love for the police or detectives round here, begging your pardon, Mr Holmes. If old Gunther is making a bit on the side most people would say 'Good Luck to you,' I reckon, and look the other way'."

Holmes gave me a quick smile as he ended his sustained impersonation.

"I went on to enquire of Gurney if he had any mail for Mr Haag awaiting delivery at the current time. For answer he went over to a bank of pigeonholes on the other side of the room and swiftly ran his hands through a number of letters and parcels. He came back with three items and handed them to me. One appeared to be a standard letter, postmarked from another part of London I knew to be heavily populated by immigrant families. The second was a flyer from a tobacco company. The third was a bulky manila envelope, Watson, heavily sealed and bound, in such a way that any attempt at tampering would have been all too apparent. The postmark showed that the latter had been sent from Southampton. I enquired of my inquisitive informant if he had been able to establish a pattern to the type of mail that Haag receives. Gurney confirmed that Haag did indeed receive a considerable amount of mail from the coast, which seemed to surprise him, but he could not give me any more incisive information."

"Thanking Gurney for his assistance I told him that I would possibly need to call on him again, and then advised him in no uncertain fashion to endeavour to forget that our recent conversations had ever taken place, and certainly not to breathe a word of what had been discussed to anybody. I could see that Gurney was taken aback by my stern tone and unequivocal directive, but he muttered his agreement. I suspect he was revelling in his confidential disclosures and wanted to further investigate the affairs of the mysterious Mr Haag. Sensing that the interview was nearly over, my informant looked to close the conversation on a beneficial note. 'It's me that could lose me job over letting you in here today. Took a risk, I did,' he wheedled."

"The stance of my informant, looking to one side and hovering on one foot, convinced me that some form of remuneration would be required to secure the assistance of Gurney in future. I slipped him a small *porboire*. I also told him that I would reach him through Wiggins again if required. 'And one more thing,' I said as Wiggins and I prepared to leave the premises. 'Were one to retain a *post restante* facility at a main Post Office for telegrams, how long would one be able to retain this facility for?' "

"'As long as you wanted,' replied Gurney. He gave me a blackened grin. 'As long as you paid, that is'."

"I murmured my thanks and we left. Wiggins and I threaded our way back to his office and I placed him under the same strictures of security as his gap-toothed associate. Before I left I supplied him with the details of the silver and artwork so recently removed from Sir Edward's place in Belgravia. I strongly suspected that these items had already wended their way to the very neighbourhood in which we stood; the East End, with its network of yards and back alleys supporting every vice, and every dealer in stolen goods from the specialist fence to the pawnbroker who asks few questions as to the provenance of his wares. Wiggins swiftly assimilated the information and promised to put the word out to what was left of the 'Irregulars', and a few of his newer contacts. I was cautiously hopeful that the location of these items, if indeed in London, would shortly be revealed to us. I asked Wiggins to contact me in Norfolk if there was any news, if, of course, I had not pre-empted him by a return visit to town."

"What do you make of it all, Holmes?" I enquired.

Holmes sighed heavily. "Espionage, Watson, or I miss my guess. Haag's haughty visitors smack to me of shadowy figures on official business. I would be very much surprised if our Gunther Haag is not receiving German embassy officials or secret service personnel at his shop, and given the varied amount of mail he apparently receives, his upper floor must be a veritable sorting office of intelligence reports."

"Of course! Reports arriving from coastal towns, such as Southampton, which traditionally have a strong British naval presence."

"And what is the principal issue occupying the minds of the men of power in London and Berlin at the moment? The naval arms race! The British want to stop it while we still hold our naval advantage, while the Germans are desperate to compete with us. Intelligence from our naval bases and dockyards would be pure gold to a German intelligence officer."

"You did not think of opening the Southampton-stamped package currently awaiting delivery in London?" I asked.

Holmes shook his head. "No. Such an interference might leave traces and alert Mr Haag or his principals. I was also reluctant to expose Wiggins and Gurney to more than was necessary. In addition, absolutely nothing is proven against Mr Haag or, for that matter, Sir Daniel Everard. In view of my suspicions regarding the threat to the national interest I believed we could be facing, however, I rang Mycroft from a private telephone booth in a nearby Post Office after I had left Wiggins, and advised him to consider pressing for surveillance activity against the tobacco shop in Bethnal Green and at the busy Post Office on Oxford Street. I outlined my belief that the facility for receiving telegrams maintained by a Mr Frederick Mountfield could be of interest to the authorities. Mycroft will, no doubt, be able to take the required steps to have the sites placed under surveillance, or to take whatever other steps seem appropriate."

"And what about Sir Daniel Everard?" I asked.

Holmes shook his head. "Predictably, Mycroft pushed for further information regarding my suspicions, arguing that he could not press for official action without a complete case to lay before the authorities. He demanded to know all I had uncovered and any theories I was party to. I refused to be drawn, advising him to do with the material I had revealed as he saw fit, but that I would reveal nothing further until I was ready. I advised him that I did not have a complete case! This was merely work in progress, but I felt that the sites I had identified *may* be of interest to the Government, if only meriting a cursory check at this juncture. To answer your question, I withheld Sir Daniel's identity from Mycroft, for now. I assured Mycroft that I was following up leads in Norfolk, but privately I felt we had to give Sir Daniel the benefit of an interview to at least give him the opportunity to refute, or give innocent meaning to, my recent observations. If my suspicions are proved to be unfounded, I will admit as much to Mycroft. Personally, I feel I have something, what with Sir Daniel's unusual association with Gunther Haag's questionable tobacco store, and his mysterious activities of yesterday, not to mention his clearly worried and troubled state of mind. I did say to Mycroft, however, that I was not yet aware of how the leads I had recently uncovered directly related to the Sea Marge business, but I was certain that there had to be a connection."

"In any case I sent a telegram to Sir Daniel via Cromer Post Office this afternoon, just before I left London to return here, advising that I wished to interview him at home at nine o'clock tomorrow morning. As for Mycroft, he was clearly dissatisfied with the limitations I imposed with regard to the disclosure of my information, but had to accept the situation. When he realised he would get nothing further from me today, he reluctantly desisted from his entreaties. To mollify him, I promised I would keep in constant touch with him as my enquiries progressed."

I waved my arms in the air in mock defeat. "This is all well and good, Holmes, but where do all the other unfathomable aspects of this case slide into place? The activities of Sir Edward, the break-ins and the strange operatives of the other night, the thefts … it is all most baffling," I cried.

"One step at a time, my friend. Let us next see what Sir Daniel reveals under my questioning."

With that we turned in.

Chapter Five

The Blakeney Connection

At breakfast the following morning Holmes spoke briefly with Sir Edward and Lady Muster, who were both looking tired and haggard at the continued presence of the Special Branch men on their estate and the restrictions on their movements. Chief Inspector Carlisle had apparently advised them that the police presence would be reduced over the next few days, leaving a small detail to act as guard until the case was resolved. I gathered that Carlisle had not endeared himself to the Musters, demonstrating as he did an overbearing and arrogant manner, and had publicly enquired why the services of an amateur, i.e. Holmes, had been engaged. Holmes smiled broadly when he learnt of this.

"I must make it my business to compare notes with the good Chief Inspector when I see him," he stated, "and see how far he has progressed towards solving this business. I take it he is still here in Overstrand?"

"Yes," replied Sir Edward, "no doubt he will be here later. It is unfortunate that Inspector Jackson and his own men returned to London yesterday. They were far more approachable."

"However, I understand they are now involved with the London end of things. How are your enquiries proceeding, Mr Holmes?" asked Sir Edward, wearily.

Holmes took his arm warmly and smiled. "I am making some progress, Sir Edward. Rest assured that I will enlighten you as soon as I am able."

Holmes caught my eye and we casually made our excuses and left, intent on reaching Sir Daniel's property in good time for our interview, and hoping to draw little attention to ourselves as we did so.

No one was in Back Lane as Holmes and I pushed open the latched gate and advanced up the garden path of The Gables. The beds on either side of the path on which we trod showed every sign of care and nurture; how strange, I thought in this moment of potential drama, that I should be dwelling on such everyday horticultural matters.

The curtains at the front of the property were all drawn. As we reached the doorway Holmes pushed the front door gently. To my surprise it opened.

I glanced quickly at Holmes. "The maid?" I queried, *sotto voce*.

My companion shook his head. "This is her day off," Holmes whispered. "Everard let slip the information the other night."

Holmes bent down to peer through the letterbox, and then drew back. I felt suddenly tense. Holmes turned to me.

"Do you have your revolver, Watson?"

I nodded, drawing my old Webley from my coat pocket and releasing the safety catch. Holmes pulled a short-barrelled pistol from his own jacket. He motioned us inside and we passed swiftly over the threshold.

From somewhere at the back of the house a gramophone was playing a classical tune. In a moment I took in the expensive fittings in the hall, the terra-cotta floor tiles, the beautifully framed art on the walls, the crystal chandeliers and mahogany furniture. My comrade moved quickly but silently towards the source of the noise and I followed swiftly in his wake. Locating the source of the music in what appeared to be a sitting room at the rear of the house I saw Holmes pause. Approximately four feet from the doorway inside the room in question a full length mirror had been situated at such an angle as to give a clear view into the room. Holmes' gun arm, which had been poised at the ready, fell to his side. I heard a voice come from within the room.

"Come in, Mr Holmes," said Sir Daniel Everard. I followed Holmes into the room.

The long sitting room had full-length windows on one side with a view to the sea not a quarter of a mile distant. The rugs and other furnishings were of the same quality that I had observed in the hall. On one wall was a collection of antique weapons and armour, including a metal breastplate and a polearm. Sir Daniel Everard sat in an easy chair next to a small writing desk wearing a green smoking jacket over a smart shirt and trousers. A bow tie was around his neck. But he looked very ill. A sheen of perspiration gleamed on pasty white features and he seemed to be having some trouble breathing.

"Doctor," he nodded to me. Then he looked at Holmes again. "Was it the telegram?" he asked.

I could see that my companion was caught off guard by this forthright opening gambit. He proceeded carefully with the conversation. "Yes," replied Holmes gently. "I am afraid it was. I recovered the text of the missive from Cromer Post

Office shortly after you sent it. And I traced the call sign of the receiving office to a busy central Post Office in London's Oxford Street. This information is now in the possession of the appropriate authorities."

Holmes watched Sir Daniel carefully. It appeared to me that Holmes was playing a bold hand on limited cards, with the aim of enticing further information from Sir Daniel. As the exchange continued it became clear that Everard, in a confused condition, was of the belief that Holmes had discovered more than had hitherto been the case.

As these opening remarks were being delivered, Everard's breathing was becoming more laboured. "You need help," I said, moving forward.

"Stay back!" he cried hoarsely. Holmes and I both started as he picked up a long-barrelled flintlock pistol that had remained hidden on his writers desk. "It still works and it is loaded," he added. "Accurate to twenty-five yards." Then almost immediately he lowered it again, as if the weight was too much for him. "But no," he intoned. "Better this way. Poison."

He continued almost without stopping.

"Felix Massner, the man who came to your attention as Frederick Mountfield, is a German émigré who has been blackmailing me for years. It goes back to the turn of the century, the time of the Boer Wars in South Africa. At the time I had been the head of the family metals firm for fifteen years but I never possessed the business acumen of my father and grandfather before him. I was unable to expand our market share, and our imperial ventures and partnerships were beginning to suffer. I was getting desperate. Although I had sole executive control I was comparatively young, and the board were beginning to undermine me. It was then that I made the one terrible mistake of my life and I have paid for it ever since."

Sir Daniel sighed deeply and a look of pained sadness crossed his features.

"As you are no doubt aware, during the Boer War of 1898 to 1901 the Boers were supported in their struggle against the British by sympathisers within the Dutch Government and business community, who arranged for financial support and shipments of arms to be supplied to the rebels. As the mother country, it was only natural that the Boers should look to Holland for support. The British Government were all too aware of this clandestine support and so placed an embargo on exports to Holland of certain materials that could be used in weapons production; raw iron, steel, ball-bearings and so on. With my balance sheet at its very worst I was approached by an old business associate in Holland, a Dutch national, who advised me that his government would pay handsomely for my steel if I agreed to sidestep the ban on the sale of military grade raw materials. Apparently the Dutch were suffering a severe shortage of such materials, partly due to our export ban."

Sir Daniel's head fell forward onto his chest. Before I could react, he resumed his monologue. "To my shame I agreed. Due to the basic laws of supply and demand I made huge profits from my illicit trade. In two and a half years I turned my business around. From that point on Everard Steel was never again in trouble, and it went on to become the great business force it still is today. I was awarded my knighthood in 1908 as a shining example of the ideal British businessman."

"How did Massner find you out?" asked Holmes softly.

Sir Daniel carried on wearily. "The Dutch businessman who originally offered me the 1899 contract had, unbeknownst to me, links to the German Intelligence Service, the Abwehr. Massner himself started his career as an ordinary travelling medical salesman who arrived in South Africa just as the Boer Wars began. He possessed a phenomenal gift for languages and as such was employed as an interpreter by the same British authorities to whom he had tried to sell his medicines. Apparently he was so helpful at interrogating Boer prisoners of war that he received a certificate of commendation from his British employers. After the war he returned briefly to Germany, whereupon he was immediately recruited into the Abwehr who had come to learn of his exploits in South Africa. He was sent to London where he had no trouble, on the back of his previous exemplary service, in obtaining employment with the Foreign Office. As you have no doubt discovered, he is now a highly placed translator dealing with highly sensitive correspondence between London and the various capitals of Europe."

"Indeed," commented Holmes, smoothly. He glanced at me quickly.

"The Germans, thanks to my Dutch friend, knew all about my secret deals during the wars. Massner was ordered to cultivate me as a spy and threaten me with exposure if I refused. My reputation would have been in ruins. Again, to my lasting regret, I acquiesced in providing him with any information I could. He has been blackmailing me for nearly ten years. While I still worked in London I was able to provide him with useful business and economic intelligence, which he would then communicate to Berlin through the German Embassy, but as time wore on the strain of the work and the threat of exposure began to tell on my health. After a prolonged period of illness two years ago, and the sudden death of my dear wife, I took the decision to retire early and handed control of Everard Steel to my sons."

"I told Massner that my work spying for Germany against my own country had left me a broken man, and I also informed him of my decision to retire to Norfolk. To my surprise he accepted my decision with good grace, and said his silence would continue as long as I sent him reports of any useful intelligence I could obtain from East Anglia. Apparently the Germans are interested in the location of defensive installations along this coast, the army camp at Weybourne, possible beach landing sites, and so on. Even so I could not imagine what really useful information I could send him from this isolated spot. In any case I did so, submitting reports to him about six times a year, and nothing untoward came of it; until the other day. I wrote and sent my first report of the year the weekend before last. Then a few days later, on the 15th of February, Massner sent me a telegram saying that he wanted further information, and wanted to ask me some questions; all couched in innocent enough language, of course. I was wary and scared at what it meant, and did not reply straight away. Then came this business at Sir Edward's place with Special Branch men swarming all over his property. I was badly frightened. I thought something was up and I tried to make urgent contact with Massner again via our intermediary in London, a tobacco-shop owner named Haag, and I also tried to reach him directly via an emergency arrangement involving a Post Office box in London."

Sir Daniel shook his head. "Rash of me. It was clearly this communication that set you on our trail."

"Do you have a home address for Massner?" Holmes enquired softly.

Everard shook his head. "No. I sent my reports to Haag's tobacco shop in the East End of London."

Everard coughed and retched heavily, the breathing now more and more shallow. Again he waved me back with his antique pistol.

"Your last report to Massner," said Holmes sharply. "You clearly believe there to be a link between this document and the recent events and police activity at Sea Marge. If these events are related, and your activities have indeed been compromised, what do you believe was in it to cause such a visible reaction by the British authorities?"

"That is the unfathomable thing," replied Everard. "I have re-read the text of my recent despatch several times and there is nothing in there that I can see as remotely sensitive. But in any case it is all up with me. I eventually burn the copies of my reports to Massner but in this case I still have it. It is in the secret wall safe behind the only picture in the master bedroom upstairs. The combination is 0308 – the month and year of my knighthood," he smiled weakly. "Do as you will with it. My only plea is that you try as far as possible to protect my family against the consequences of my actions."

Everard's breath suddenly started to come in gasps and he lay back against his chair. I was at his side in an instant but the staring eyes and the weak, fading heartbeat told me all I needed to know. I looked at Holmes and shook my head.

"I can do nothing for him, Holmes."

"Let us obtain this report and make a swift departure," said Holmes. "What cause of death will a post-mortem on Sir Daniel's body determine?"

I noticed a small blue bottle lying on its side on Sir Daniel's desk. I swept it up and sniffed it. "It appears as if Sir Daniel has taken an overdose of a poisonous compound. A lengthy post-mortem by a competent pathologist may detect traces of it in his blood. But the most likely explanation, given his age and condition, will be a coronary failure."

"Let us hope it is the latter. Come Watson, let us further Sir Daniel's dying request and also further our own investigation by removing that report. It would be as well if we vacated this building before the discovery of the late Knight's body."

Close to the spot where I had found the blue bottle I noticed a small brown envelope addressed to Holmes in Sir Daniel's hand. It was propped up against an inkwell. I passed it to my friend.

Holmes turned and made as if to leave the room, before something caught his attention on the writer's bureau and he checked himself sharply. He swept up a small document and waved it at me.

"My telegram of yesterday." He pocketed it swiftly. "There is a chance our presence here will not be established. I sent my telegram to the Cromer Post Office, rather than Overstrand, where it may have come within the purview of all those Special Branch policemen."

I pocketed the blue bottle I had recently sniffed. "So now we lay ourselves open to a charge of removing police evidence from a crime scene," I sighed.

"Crime scene?" My companion feigned surprise. "This man took his own life, Watson."

"Suicide is still illegal," I reminded him, "and in light of the strange circumstances surrounding his death I believe our legal position would be considered somewhat thin."

Holmes grinned suddenly. "We have trod a similarly fine legal line in pursuit of the greater goal before, Watson. Have you forgotten the Milverton affair?"

I grimaced again. Holmes was referring to a case over twenty years old, at the conclusion of which he and I were forced to don cracksman's garb to effect entry into the Hampstead home of a villainous blackmailer, Charles Augustus Milverton, in order to remove sensitive documents pertaining to the personal circumstances of our client, Lady Eva Brackwell. By the end of the evening Milverton was dead by the hand of one of his earlier victims and the aforementioned documents destroyed by ourselves. In a case Holmes took most personally, he decided to withhold his knowledge of the incident from the police officers investigating Milverton's death on the grounds that moral justice had been served.

I opened my mouth to retort but Holmes had already turned on his heel and was moving swiftly from the room. With a final glance at Sir Daniel, I followed.

Minutes later saw Holmes and myself hurrying down Back Lane clasping a large buff envelope, liberated from Sir Daniel's safe, that contained a copy of the final missive that Sir Daniel had communicated to Felix Massner in London. At the bottom of Back Lane a short path led up to a hillock overlooking the sea upon which was situated a bench for the enjoyment of the view. Again, the whole area was deserted. Stealing a glance around, Holmes extracted the report and began to read. Dated February 10th, the document appeared to my way of thinking to offer precious little useful information. The recent social events in Overstrand and Cromer were described and Sir Daniel had gained the intelligence that a division of troops would be exercising presently near Weybourne Camp. Towards the end of the document reference was made to the comings and goings of Mr Churchill, the fact that he was due to come up to Overstrand by sea on the battleship the *Queen Mary* and two fishing boats, the *Misty Jane* and the *Yarmouth Adventuress* (his usual choice) would bring him and his family and retainers ashore. I started in surprise as I realised that these were the fishing vessels I had read about so recently in Cromer, the two that had been lost at sea earlier in the month. The report was signed 'Raven' – presumably the codename employed by Everard during his communications with Massner.

"There appears to be a lot in this report about the comings and goings of Mr Churchill," I commented. "You do not think we should fear an attempt on his life, do you Holmes?"

Holmes steepled his hands under his chin and gazed at the sky.

"I think that ... unlikely. To what end? Mr Churchill is First Sea Lord ... a military role. He is not in the business of shaping or directing Government policy, as he was during his tenure as Home Secretary a couple of years ago. Nevertheless it stands to reason that Massner wanted elaboration on *something* in this report. This report was written on a Saturday. Even were it sent to Haag's tobacco emporium on the same day, we can reasonably expect that the contents only came within the purview of Felix Massner on Tuesday at the earliest. And yet a telegram requesting further information is despatched from Massner to Everard on the Thursday. Hmm. Massner's action would seem to suggest a degree of urgency on his part."

Holmes looked at the paper in front of him again.

"There is a comment here about the movement of troops? What of it, Watson? Weybourne camp is well known as a military training ground ... troops come and go from there frequently. I remember from reading a booklet on the local history of the area that Weybourne is renowned for the deep water immediately off the coast; a fact that has alarmed British national defence officials since the time of the Spanish Armada. Clearly were we facing an imminent German invasion then details of a military presence at Weybourne would be a useful piece of information. But such a consideration does not stand up at the present time, even given the strained diplomatic situation. The only item here that is remotely intriguing is the reference to these two fishing boats that Churchill uses as a ferry service. You yourself ascertained that they were both sunk in accidents at sea, recently, within a few days of each other."

"Open this," instructed Holmes, who fished in his pocket and handed me the letter addressed to him that had lain unobtrusively upon Everard's desk. Swiftly I was able to confirm that it contained a written confession along the lines of that which we had heard during Everard's final and dramatic revelations. It confirmed in writing that Massner, alias Mountfield, and Haag were agents of the German Intelligence Service, and stated the address of the latter's shop in London that Holmes had already surveyed. In the letter Sir Daniel also referred us to his wall safe, whence we found the incriminating report.

Holmes had adopted a faraway look. He spoke after several minutes.

"Well, Watson, we are beginning to be faced with more questions than answers!" My colleague pondered briefly again and then began to speak in a measured way.

"I have already supplied Mycroft with sufficient information to begin the task of dismantling the spy ring of which Sir Daniel was a member. I am convinced that he will know the best course of action to follow in this regard, and that the correct results will be obtained by the appropriate authorities. Sir Daniel's dying request to us was to try to protect his family as far as possible from the repercussions of his treasonous actions. Always assuming that the network of which he was a member is duly eradicated, and any damage perpetrated is assessed and contained by the relevant authorities, personally I see no reason why information regarding Sir Daniel's guilt should be widely broadcast. I will have to clear things with Mycroft, but it may be that the information can be kept from his family, or if this proves impossible, at least restricted to his immediate relatives and kept from the wider public. As a peer of the realm there will be a desire in Whitehall to preserve his reputation unsullied, of that I am certain. Furthermore, the revelation of the existence of a spy deep in the heart of the Foreign Office will be treated very secretively and gingerly, I am sure, and an attempt to conceal the one issue will go hand-in-hand with the other."

"I think as far as Sir Daniel is concerned the best course of action will be to allow the discovery of his body during the natural turn of events. The initial diagnosis, at least, should be death by natural causes. You were correct, Watson, when you alleged we had committed a felony by removing this incriminating evidence from Sir Daniel's house. But I will convey the material to Mycroft shortly, and I will manage the consequences of our temporary retention of the report at that time. There are other outstanding issues that command our attention, and we may need this report to pursue them. I would rather go to Mycroft with a complete summary when we have all the facts at our disposal, rather than at this juncture with a number of issues unresolved."

"There is still the business at Sea Marge and Halkin Place, and my personal promise to Sir Edward and Lady Muster to see the case through to the end. Frankly, Watson, despite the coincidence in timing, and the obvious fears of Everard, whose nerves were in any case as frayed as old rope, I see no *direct* connection between his treasonous activities and the raid and subsequent Special Branch investigation at Sea Marge. If the police had suspected him of anything they would have been here. No, there is something else, something more to this business. The more I consider it, the greater difficulty I have accepting that the Germans or their sympathisers have the personnel upon these shores capable of carrying out the escapades and derring-do that occurred at Sir Edward's properties the other evening. It is simply not credible to imagine that people such as Everard and his colleagues, whose very anonymity and activities depend upon secrecy, had the resources or the detailed knowledge to mount such brazen operations. You will remember that we have obtained some limited evidence pointing to the Sea Marge operation, at least, being carried out by men of some nautical affiliation. I see no such possible link in the Everard-Massner-Haag fraternity! Besides, you could tell from our recent interview with Sir Daniel that he was as much in the dark about the business at Muster's as anyone else."

I could see that Holmes was torn in deciding which course of action to pursue next. He looked again at the report Everard had sent to Massner, then slowly and deliberately stabbed his finger down on the text.

"These fishing boats. I wonder, Watson ..."

A few seconds later and my colleague stood rapidly, his mind made up. "I will speak to my brother with my conclusions and findings to date when I am back in London, pursuing the outstanding leads I have in the city. I am referring to the forthcoming interviews I have with Mr

Radley, the photographic specialist in New Oxford Street, and Wiggins, over the possible dispersal of the stolen goods from Halkin Place into the East End criminal community. In the meantime … there may be nothing in it … I think I will make a few inquiries into the provenance of these fishing vessels that disappeared so recently. There appears to be some rather unusual coincidences surrounding their loss, and it seems clear that Mr Massner was particularly interested in *something* in Everard's last report. From a number of minor references, I would say that this was it."

"Have you an idea how the Opium Conference may fit into all of this?" I asked.

"Back of my mind, Watson, at the back of my mind!" my friend replied, smiling.

Like a man reinvigorated, Holmes tucked away the papers in the voluminous folds of his long overcoat and we began to descend rapidly from the hill. The entire area was deserted.

"I believe these boats were berthed a little way along the coast," I commented as we moved.

"The harbour-master's office in Cromer," said Holmes. "They will be able to advise us of all the ports of registry along this stretch of coast, and may even have records of all local vessels. In any case, the loss of two boats within such a narrow time period will no doubt have provoked discussion among the local maritime community. I will be staggered if he cannot assist us."

We set off towards the little railway halt of Overstrand barely half a mile distant with the intention of disembarking at Cromer Beach and seeking out the offices of the Port Authority. The morning was advancing and a fresh, chill wind was driving in off the sea. Out to sea the white tips on the waves were being whipped up by the wind. As luck would have it Holmes and I had a short wait of barely a few minutes before a local train service arrived, which duly deposited us at Cromer station five minutes later. It did not take us long to locate the local harbour-master's office, which was to the east of the town, a surprisingly small office overlooking a slipway from which the Cromer steam lifeboat would be launched when her services were required. Further along the beach a line of crab boats were drawn up away from high water.

Upon entering the small, whitewashed office Holmes and I were forced to navigate a couple of small chairs and a table upon which lay every conceivable form of nautical document, before finding ourselves in front of a desk at which sat a physically trim man wearing a nondescript white sweater and iron-rimmed spectacles. One entire side of his office wall was covered by an enormous chart depicting the Norfolk coastline, highlighting current direction, sea depths and natural hazards, including the notorious sandbanks known as the Haisbro' Sands. A barometer was affixed to the wall behind him. I glanced at his desk and saw papers governing various maritime matters such as the repair and repositioning of buoys offshore, maintenance of the Cromer lifeboat, and so on. Interspersed loosely with this paperwork was all manner of paraphernalia such as defunct oil lamps and bits of old rope.

Finally he looked up as we stood before his desk and a pair of friendly eyes regarded us from an intelligent, weather-beaten face. "Can I help you?" he asked, in a measured Norfolk drawl.

"My name is Sherlock Holmes, and this is my colleague, Dr Watson," began Holmes pleasantly. "We were hoping that you may be able to offer us some assistance."

"Ah," said the port master, holding out his hand. "You'll be here on account of the business at Sir Edward's place. It's all over the local papers."

"That is so," replied Holmes smoothly. "However, as part of the ... wider circumstances surrounding this enquiry, I was hoping to unearth some of the facts surrounding the recent loss of the two fishing boats from along the coast."

The man looked at us quizzically, and then sighed, as if it was not for him to question the business of the great Sherlock Holmes. "A rum affair, that one. Lost two boats in forty-eight hours. We still don't know what really happened."

"Perhaps you could tell me all you do know," replied my friend.

"Well ... let me see." Our friend opened a desk drawer and after a moment's rustling he brought out a buff coloured file. Inside I could see newspaper clippings and other notes.

"First was the *Yarmouth Adventuress*, an eighty foot herring drifter which vanished, we think, somewhere off the Dutch coast after heading out to the Terschelling fishing grounds. There has been no trace or sighting of her and what befell her is a mystery. This is unusual in that the short stretch of water between here and Holland is normally thick with English and Dutch fishing vessels of every description, 'specially recently, what with the boom harvest in herring and mackerel we have had over the last couple of years. We would have expected a sighting or report of some nature."

"When was this?" asked Holmes. "Also, what can you tell me about her design and history?"

The port master stretched back in his chair and looked again at his notes. "Common steam drifter of a type to be found all around the coast from Hunstanton to Lowestoft. Nothing remarkable."

"And Great Yarmouth was her home port?" persisted Holmes.

"Originally, yes. But at the time of her disappearance she was fishing out of Blakeney, just along the coast. She was bought last year by a group of businessmen from down south … London I believe. I don't know how much you know about the Norfolk fishing business, Mr Holmes, but it is very rare for fishermen, even a group, to own a fishing smack outright. Usually they are hired to man and fish the boats by the owners who pay their crew a share of the profits from fish landed. And as I said earlier, there is a lot of interest in the market just now from both local businessmen, and those from afar, due to the buoyant state of the mackerel and herring industry and the profits to be had."

"When was this?" repeated Holmes.

Our friend replied without consulting his notes. "She left Blakeney on the morning of the 10th of February. Nothing was seen of her thereafter."

"You are being most helpful. Could we now trouble you for some details of the other boat?"

The first buff file was placed back in the drawer and another one took its place on our friend's desk.

"The *Misty Jane,* also sailing out of Blakeney. Lost on the afternoon of the 11th of February. In this case we do know what happened to her. She was destroyed by a fire just outside the entrance to Blakeney channel."

"Design?"

"Fifty-foot sailing trawler. At least she originally relied on sail but I understand from my counterpart in the Blakeney harbour-master's office that she had recently had one of those new-fangled internal combustion engines fitted. Paraffin-driven, I understand."

"Hmm. That could explain the fire. What about loss of life in these accidents?"

The Cromer man shrugged. "We do not know exactly who was aboard either boat. No bodies have been recovered from the Blakeney accident by the coastguard. The fishermen crewing both vessels were not local men, so the local community can offer few insights into their next of kin."

"Not local men," echoed Holmes. "Is that normal?"

"Not unusual. We get Scotsmen, Dutchmen and fishermen from all over England along this coast, fishing 'king herring'. It is rumoured that these men came from Kent or Sussex way; down south at any rate. Both of the boats lost were working for the same firm, so I gather they are dealing with identifying next of kin."

"*Both* boats were working for the same firm?" said Holmes, surprised.

"Yes. I haven't the name, but I'm sure my colleague along the coast will be able to help you further."

"My thanks to you once more. We will progress our enquiry further in Blakeney. A couple of final points. Who is managing the enquiry into the losses? The local police, I presume, with the assistance of the coastguard?"

"As I understand it, yes. I would think a report would be prepared for the district coroner in due course."

"My friend and I understand that these boats were sometimes used by Mr Churchill to ferry himself and his family from an Admiralty warship to the foot of Overstrand steps. Is that correct?"

"Yes, that's an open secret in Cromer. The vessels were sometimes used for that purpose, true enough. They would come up to the beach and then Churchill and his party would use a small boat to row the last few yards ashore. He has been doing this for some years, particularly in summer, but has greater opportunity now as he is First Sea Lord and commands the navy's resources. I believe he had been using these particular fishing boats to run him ashore for the past six months or so."

"How did Churchill meet the crews?"

"There's no secret there. Churchill is very personable and mixes very well with the local people, particularly the local fishermen. He is often seen chatting with the crab boat fishermen at the bottom of Overstrand cliffs when he is up this way. He seems to be genuinely interested in their livelihood. He has a fondness for art, I believe, and sometimes uses the fishermen and their boats in his studies when he is relaxing here on holiday."

"But you mentioned just now that the crews of these particular boats do not come from among the local populace?"

The port master shrugged. "That is so. Perhaps he knows them from his home county. Mr Churchill has a home in Kent, does he not?"

Holmes changed tack. "Where is Blakeney?"

For a reply our contact stood up and went to the map on the far wall. He picked up a pointer and rested it on a spit of land stretching out to sea some seven miles west of our current position.

"This is Blakeney Point. This spit shelters a number of small ports inland. Blakeney is at the base of a winding channel … here" – his pointer moved slightly as he found his new destination. "The closest railway station is Holt, on the Cromer to Norwich line via Melton Constable."

"Our thanks to you once more." Holmes bowed courteously. "You have been most helpful."

"I could telephone my Blakeney counterpart to advise him to expect you?" said the man, indicating a telephone I had not previously observed perched in an alcove behind him.

"Thank you, that would be kind. We will join him for a late luncheon." We left the office as our friend lifted the telephone receiver. Swiftly, we negotiated the heart of Cromer and were shortly thereafter boarding a train destined for the small market town of Holt.

As our rustic three-carriage steam train left the station Holmes spoke for the first time since leaving the harbour-masters office.

"Upon my word, Watson, there are some odd coincidences surrounding the disappearance of these fishing boats. Both lost, we understand, within twenty-four hours of each other in entirely different circumstances, both operated by the same company, and both utilised by Mr Churchill as a personal waterborne ferry service when he could, one suspects, call on the services of crab fishermen far closer to home from Cromer or Overstrand. This avenue of enquiry may yet have legs!"

Chapter Six

Secrets of the *Misty Jane*

$\mathbf{T}$he little train ran through the attractive Norfolk countryside, stopping at picturesque halts along the way, and dawdled a while at the halt of Weybourne, from where we had a fine view out to sea. The village with its ancient church, windmill and red-tiled flint cottages was framed against the skyline. To the left stood Weybourne army camp, with its garrison of soldiers and units of heavy artillery keeping a watch upon this stretch of coast. As we were discovering, the ongoing political tensions with Germany meant that sites such as Weybourne, with its deep water offshore and smooth beaches to aid an invasion force, were assuming a greater importance than had been the case only a few years previously.

Twenty minutes later saw Holmes and I deposited on Holt station, which appeared to be an adequate terminus for a North Norfolk market town. Two twin-gabled brick station buildings faced each other across the tracks, and sundry buildings included a large water tower, several lock-up sheds and small warehouses for goods storage, and a number of cattle pens to restrain these animals prior to their transport to market.

On the station forecourt Holmes and I were fortunate enough to engage the services of a Mr Ben Empson, local purveyor of carriages for hire, and on this occasion seated in a small trap behind a fine pair of chestnut mares. Before long Holmes had negotiated a fare for the journey to the small port of Blakeney, five miles distant, and we set out through countryside covered with farmers' fields in various states of employ. Here and there we espied farm labourers employed in dipping sheep, or threshing corn with the aid of a huge steam-driven traction engine.

Before long we crested a rise and saw, in the distance, the sea once more, and Mr Empson began the descent into the small port of Blakeney. We travelled slowly down the unmade high street, passing typical Norfolk flint and red-tiled cottages, and here and there a building exceeding two stories in height with curving Dutch-style gables. Soon I noticed a multitude of gulls and other seabirds wheeling and crying in the skies above us, and the salty tang in the fresh coastal air blowing in off the sea. The street, which had been quiet as we entered the village at the top of the hill, became more busy and noisy as our party progressed downwards towards the quay and the waterfront. Collapsing tables were laid outside certain shops and wares were laid out for the perusal of local ladies who were investigating all manner of goods for sale including crockery and woollens. I noticed a blacksmith and a cobbler doing a steady trade.

We disembarked from Mr Empson's conveyance at the bottom of the high street where the gradient levelled to reveal a small quay in a roughly horseshoe pattern. To our immediate left stood substantial flint warehouses offering a storage facility for coal, timber, grain and other exportable commodities. Tied up at the quay were several fine twin-mast sailing vessels and an impressive steam freighter, smoke lazily drifting from her funnel and offering an acrid taint to the chill air. Fishermens' huts were much in evidence, drying nets stretched out on their roofs, and in front of these same huts were their owners, mending nets or preparing pitch and tar to seal the bottoms of the crab-boats and oyster-dredgers hauled up on a mud bank to the right of the main quay. The loading and unloading of cargo was taking place all along the small quay. Shouts and whistles, the neigh of horses, and the blast of steam whistles all contributed to the small hive of marine activity that I was witnessing.

I was jerked from my reverie by Holmes, who indicated a building just up the hill from our current position, and to the right.

"The harbour-master's offices, and the coastguard," said Holmes. "That is our next destination, Watson."

A set of steps wound up to a first floor office with a wonderful view of the quay and thence out over the estuary to the spit and open sea. The offices of this, the Blakeney harbour-master, Mr Andrew Cook, were essentially similar to those of his Cromer counterpart. The same preponderance of charts was in evidence, and on desks and tables were documents pertaining to the running of a small fishing and trading community. I noticed papers concerned with the pay and organisation of local pilots, collection of dues on traders, and, again, documents concerned with the running of Blakeney lifeboat. Mr Cook, we learnt, was both harbour-master and the senior coastguard official in Blakeney. Our new contact looked up from a map he had been studying in one corner of the room as we knocked and entered.

"Mr Holmes and Dr Watson," said Cook, who was consuming what I took to be tea from a mug as he moved away from his maps to greet us. "Old Jack Arlow over at Cromer rang me to say that you would be visiting. You've come to see me about that smack what was lost off the Point?"

"Correct, Mr Cook," said Holmes smiling. "Anything you can tell us to further our understanding of what happened to both the vessels lost from this port recently, would be of immeasurable assistance."

"Are you with the police, or what?" Cook asked suddenly.

Holmes stole me a quick glance. "My colleague and I are operating in an entirely independent capacity. Anything you would be good enough to share with us will remain utterly confidential. I would not presume to disclose to the police anything that was entrusted to me in confidence. You may perhaps have heard of my small reputation as a private detective in London? On many occasions during the investigation of a case the foundations of my success were due to a trusted informant, whose confidences I would never have been so base, or indeed foolhardy, to reward with betrayal."

Holmes paused before continuing with his next question. "Can I enquire why you asked?"

Cook shook his head and waved his hand, as if to dismiss his earlier comment.

"Constable Spence in Holt is doing the paperwork on what happened, Mr Holmes. I don't pretend to know the ins and outs of it, but there's something odd. Bert Spence and I, we normally work well together, but he's become evasive over this business. Things don't seem to be moving much on the enquiry, Mr Holmes, but I'm ready to help with a report for the coroner. It's as if Spence doesn't want to move things on, for some reason. I wondered whether you might have been called in to give the investigation some fresh legs, shall we say."

"Noted. However, we are not acting in an official capacity," replied Homes at length. "Let us say no more of it."

Mr Cook began to relax.

"Are you hungry?" he asked. A quick glance at my pocket watch advised me it was nearly two o'clock and my colleague and I had taken no sustenance since an early breakfast.

Over tea and Norfolk ham rolls purchased from a vendor close to his offices, Cook went deeper into the circumstances surrounding the losses of the *Yarmouth Adventuress* and the *Misty Jane*. In truth he could not add much to the bald facts surrounding the former's disappearance that we had gathered in Cromer. We soon discovered, however, that there was more to the loss of the *Misty Jane* than we had thus far uncovered.

Our man confirmed that the boat in question was a fifty-foot sailing trawler that had recently, the previous autumn, had a paraffin-driven internal combustion engine fitted by her new owners. He further confirmed that the Blakeney lifeboat sailed to the assistance of a distressed vessel when smoke was spotted at the estuary mouth, but by the time the lifeboat arrived at the place where the accident happened the *Misty Jane* had sunk. No bodies were recovered from the wreck, although a few small pieces of charred wreckage had been subsequently recovered.

"Who owned her?" asked Holmes, withdrawing his notebook and propelling pencil from his jacket pocket.

"A firm from London called Mendel & Newcombe. They don't keep no offices up here, like the local merchants. There's nothing odd about that ... 'king herring' has done well for us over the last couple of years and many businessmen from other parts of the country want a slice of the pie."

"But surely they must have a representative who conducts arrangements with the fishermen, arranges fish sales, transport to markets, and so on?" queried Holmes. "Since the occurrence of these two tragedies has a representative not been present to assess the loss of these assets, not to mention offer help in liaising with and supporting the victims' families? The fishermen crewing the *Misty Jane* and the other missing vessel, which I now understand also belonged to Mendel & Newcombe, were Kent or Sussex men, I believe?"

"Yes, no and yes," replied our man absently. "Yes, a man from the company *has* been up here sometimes, normally on a monthly basis, to give orders to his crews and leave instructions with me over fish landing and tariffs and procedures. Mr Naylor is a big hard man, Mr Holmes, with big ham like fists and a red flash below his right eye. He looks a tough sort to me. I'd hazard he ain't always been in a pleasant line of work." At this juncture I noticed Holmes raise an eyebrow and glance at me. Our friend, however, continued without stopping. "But he pays all his company dues on time, right enough, and I can't say we've ever had any trouble with him, or his people, as traders and merchants in this port. Its odd, mind, but we've not seen him or anyone else from Mendel & Newcombe since these events. The police in Holt, who are handling the inquiry like I said, sent me a telegram stating that they were dealing with this company direct on the matters of informing relatives, gathering information for the coroner's report, and so on."

Cook paused briefly and then continued.

"Yes to your third question, Mr Holmes ... his crews are all from the south, Kent way I think, not that I really know. They keep themselves to themselves they do, don't really mix with the local lads at all. Don't drink much in the local pubs or anything. They are polite to talk to, mind ... although they can find some ripe language if they find you snooping around their boats. But generally they just get on with a bit of fishing and landing moderate catches ... though they could do better, and land more often, to my mind, Mr Holmes, what with their fancy gear. These are, or were, good boats, Mr Holmes. These people keep a couple of small warehouses under lock and key just around the quay, and sometimes I see small carts from Holt station unloading the Lord knows what there ... crates and so on. Can't see what they would be storing there. I asked Mr Naylor once what they kept in there and he just replied 'stores'. Well! Naylor did infer that his boats would engage in a little bit of trade with the Low Countries to supplement his fishing interests, you know, when the fish are out of season, but I can't see it myself. We were all a bit curious at first but after a while it all settled down and now nobody pays them any mind. As to this sinking business, normally a fishing community is struck to the core when a boat goes down, but we just don't know much about these fellows so the whole feel is just a bit awkward."

Holmes had been listening and making notes intently. "Do you have any further details for this Mr Naylor?"

Cook shook his head. "Not really. I have his business address in the City of London but no more."

He passed Holmes a business ledger from which my friend made a rapid note.

"Do you know who were aboard these vessels during the events in question?" asked Holmes.

Cook produced a sheet of paper on which were written a list of names. "One of the crew from another of Mendel &

Newcombe's boats, the *Pearl*, gave me this list of those supposedly aboard the two boats during the time in question. Mind you, I've only his word for it. I couldn't tell you for definite who was aboard at the time; no-one could, I reckon."

He handed the list to Holmes who duly made some more notes. From my vantage point sitting next to Holmes there appeared to be two lists comprising three and five names respectively.

"And the crewman who provided you with this information, where may he be found?"

"His name is Marks ... I don't know his first name. Try around the quay to the far left; that's where the *Pearl* is laid up, and where the other two were moored before they disappeared. Other than that you could try the lodging rooms above the King's Arms public house ... I think some of those fellows lodge there. I haven't seen many of them around recently, though, at least not since the accidents."

"And these singular warehouses, with their mysterious holdings. These may be found around the quay too?"

Cook nodded. "There are two standing alone just to the side of the *Pearl*. Those are the ones."

"When did this company begin fishing from Blakeney?" asked Holmes.

"Last autumn."

"And finally, you mentioned that some wreckage was recovered from the site of the *Misty Jane* incident. Has this been retained?"

"Yes, in case it needs to be examined for the coroners report. If it ever happens," he added ruefully.

"May we be permitted to see it?"

"Don't see as it can do any harm," he said hesitantly "Just for ten minutes."

Our friend led us out into the street and we turned right, walking around the quay a short distance to a sturdy storage hut protected by a padlock. He let us in and flung the doors wide open to make the most of the natural light. The afternoon had turned grey and Cook lit an oil lamp in case we had to probe into the recesses of the debris recovered from the unfortunate *Misty Jane*.

Some timber planks covered the floor and on top of these rested what appeared, to my untrained eye, to be the remains of a covered structure and some strakes from what I took to be the stern of the vessel. I could just identify, through the grime and blackened, stressed woodwork, some letters of her name and homeport picked out in white. Some boxes on the floor held small items recovered from the wreck site.

Holmes was already on one knee, magnifying glass in hand, studying the covered structure.

He turned briefly to our guide. "Wheelhouse?"

"It is indeed, Mr Holmes. You can see the fire damage along one side. For my money I reckon the paraffin motor did the damage." He swept out an arm to include all the contents of the hut. "This is all that we recovered. Most of it came ashore on the spit. She must have burned fierce," he said, dolefully.

Holmes did not reply. He was gingerly tracing a line with his fingers down the tortured and scarred timber of the remains of the wheelhouse. At a certain point near where the base of the wheelhouse would have sat flush with the deck the blackening of the wood became more pronounced, with heavy charring apparent.

"Tell me, Cook, would her new engine have been situated below the wheelhouse?"

"Ah, not far off," Cook conceded. "'Least I ain't seen many boats with this type of conversion, but that's my understanding of it."

"Only this heat damage is clearly extensive and penetrating. In my experience this type of stress and trauma is not inconsistent with an explosion. Do you believe the paraffin engine could have exploded and caused this disaster?"

"Well now, Mr Holmes." The port master gave my friend a sidelong glance. "I've been around boats all my life. I admit I've less experience of the new steam and motor engines than some, but I'll tell you this. The lifeboat was away down Blakeney estuary ten minutes after the smoke was spotted. My number two skippered her." He waved his arm airily back in the direction of the office, with its excellent vantage point of the estuary and beyond. "Why do you think the coastguard lookout is situated where it is? Many a life has been saved by a quick lifeboat launch after a sighting of a vessel in distress from up there. In this case the lifeboat was at the site in twenty minutes. The fishing boat had already gone to the bottom in that time. Now in every other fire case I have known, the vessel burns for hours, if not days, before sinking. I would say that the paraffin could have burnt her out, given time, but I reckon she was crippled and sunk by something else. And as you say, an explosion in the engine seems the most likely cause."

"Hmm," muttered Holmes. He stayed for another ten minutes examining the wreckage before straightening and shaking the port master's hand.

"Thank you for your assistance." We turned to leave and left the shed.

"You will let me know if you find out anything else?" called our friend.

Holmes merely waved as the latter closed the doors and began to lock away the wreckage from the *Misty Jane*.

"If I can," muttered Holmes almost inaudibly, "if I can."

We headed left around the quay. "Come Watson. We still have time to interview Mr Marks and have a look at this other Mendel & Newcombe vessel, the *Pearl*, not to mention those singular storage facilities."

"What do you make of it all, Holmes?" I asked as we walked.

"There is something seriously amiss here, Watson. I have not spent all my time since my retirement just keeping bees you know! I have kept abreast of developments in forensic examination, and the study of crime scenes, thanks to an instructor in new techniques at Scotland Yard. One of the fields I have looked at is the development of explosives. I am reasonably clear in my own mind that the woodwork of that vessel exhibited properties consistent with exposure to an explosive device. The timber of the wheelhouse showed clear evidence of such trauma."

"She was sunk deliberately?" I stammered, amazed.

"On the evidence I have recently reviewed, I believe that to be a virtual certainty," answered my friend grimly. "The *why* is the next inevitable question. Let us hurry."

This last was prompted by a light drizzle that began to fall gently as we walked around the quay, causing us to draw up our overcoat collars tightly as we walked. My mind was in turmoil at the implications of Holmes' last revelation. We headed to the far left of the quay, following Cook's directions. Before long the activity and noise around the hub of the quay had died away, and we found ourselves alone, scrambling along a muddy bank, taking care so as to keep our footing and avoid falling headlong into the filthy waters of the channel, or onto one of the dank smelling fishing craft moored alongside the bank. Here and there gantries and wooden steps gave access to the decks of these craft. The reek of dead fish filled our nostrils. To our left lifting derricks, small warehouses and granary stores appeared as hazy shadows in the grey, rainy winter gloom. To our right, beyond the channel and the fishing craft, stretched a vast expanse of salt marshes.

After about seventy yards of negotiating old fishing nets, crab pots, and a number of upended boats, Holmes and I encountered the stern of what I took to be a herring drifter drawn up on railings out of the water. Holmes pointed to her stern. 'Pearl, Blakeney' was visible high above the water line. Even from my position I could see her steam funnel, along with the main and mizzen masts. I estimated that she was about seventy feet long. Just to one side of her were the two small huts that Cook had mentioned, their black timbers and lack of windows giving them a slightly sinister appearance. In a minute Holmes had performed a circuit around these huts and was back alongside me.

"Sturdy construction, Watson. No windows and two formidable padlocks upon each door. What are our friends so anxious to shield from prying eyes?"

Holmes scanned the *Pearl* and pointed down the side of the vessel. I soon saw what he had spotted – a ladder leading up to the deck from the bank near her bow. We moved up to the ladder and in no time at all my friend had scaled it and I saw him disappear from my view on to the deck. I warily guarded the ladder and kept casting about me for possible danger but the entire area seemed to be deserted.

It can only have been five minutes, but it felt much longer, before I saw my friend descending back down the ladder towards me.

"Well?"

Holmes blew on his hands. "I could not find anything untoward but there was something strange about the design of her hatchways. The fish hold, nets and sails holds, and stores all have hatchways reinforced with what appears to be steel, and, again, very strong padlocks. A somewhat unusual level of security for a standard fishing vessel, wouldn't you say, Watson? Perhaps fish is not the only commodity these boats have been transporting."

"Indeed. Smuggling?" I queried.

Holmes shrugged. "The boat seemed to be deserted. If I could have but spoken with our mysterious Mr Marks, perhaps we could have learnt a little more."

No sooner had these words left my friend's mouth than a challenging shout reached us from the deck above. We both looked up instinctively to see a man jumping over the *Pearl*'s gunwale and falling heavily to the ground in front of us. But he did not land badly. On the contrary he landed perfectly on his feet, knees flexing to cushion the impact of the short drop, and in the next fluid motion he had straightened and was swiftly closing the distance to Holmes and myself. He was dressed in dark oilskin trousers and a dark blue fisherman's jersey and wore a woollen cap. His face was set and his eyes were like chips of granite as he advanced in a measured way, purposefully swinging what appeared to be an iron bar, or possibly a nautical tool doubling as a makeshift weapon. He reached Holmes first and aimed a blow at his head that Holmes managed to avoid but in so doing lost his balance, causing him to slip and fall to the ground near the exposed keel.

"Marks!" my friend shouted, causing the newcomer to pause momentarily. But by this time I had reached into my coat pocket and drawn my Webley revolver, releasing the safety catch and covering the man.

"Drop the weapon!" I barked.

His reaction surprised me. In one overarm motion he went on the offensive, hurling the bar at me with venomous force, the weapon spinning end over end until it crashed against the underside of the boat, inches from my right forearm. I moved to avoid the missile, and when I looked back at my assailant I was just in time to see him rolling under the boat before making his escape through the maze of upturned boats, crab-pots, nets, and other marine clutter on the other side of the *Pearl*.

As I went to help Holmes up he cried "Hands, Watson, hands!" in a celebratory tone. I looked down at my hand and forearm in bewilderment. Had the villain wounded me, I wondered?

Holmes snorted as I helped him up. "Not *your* hands! Did you see *his* hands? Strong and active, yes, but a fisherman? Never! The hands of a fisherman show all manner of cuts, scars, callouses, and every type of manual injury thanks to a lifetime of working with nets. I could see no such affliction on the hands of *that* fine fellow. Yet he was obviously very fit, and lethal with it. A military man, Watson, a naval man, or I miss my guess. Come, it is beginning to get dark. We would never catch our man now, in this environment, even if we were of a mind to attempt it. Let us see if we can gather any further clues as to the nature and business of our mysterious assailant at the lodging house these people apparently use.

The King's Arms it was called, was it not? Quickly now! We can suppose that our erstwhile assailant will give us a short period of time to clear the area, time we can use wisely to make a quick reconnaissance of his lodgings."

We located the whitewashed King's Arms swiftly enough, at the same end of the village from whence we had so recently ventured down the quay to the encounter beside the *Pearl*. A smoky bar on the ground floor was being patronised, despite the early hour, by half a dozen fisher-types in the ubiquitous jersey sweaters and contributing to the smoky atmosphere through the liberal use of clay pipes and noxious 'baccies'. Holmes peered around the doorway to the bar, seemingly confirmed our man was not *in situ*, and then, in a flash, was behind an alcove clearly used as the guest reception, scanning the register.

"Number four for our bird, Dr Watson," he whispered, before heading for the stairs and ascending them three at a time, long overcoat swirling around him. I hurried after him.

"Do we not require the key?" I whispered, as I caught up with him on the first floor landing.

Holmes dipped into his coat and, for reply, produced a small leather wallet that he flipped open, revealing skeleton keys, small jemmies, spikes, and the like – in fact all the tools of the trade for a professional cracksman.

"If we are quick about it, Watson, we can perform a comprehensive search of our friend's room and be gone within minutes. If he returned and saw his key missing he would at the very least look up the landlady, and any semblance of secrecy we maintain could well be compromised."

"Or he may dispense with the services of the landlady and put his shoulder to the door instead," I grumbled, to no reaction from my companion.

Room number four proved, like so many of those in our nation's cheaper hostelries, to have no lock worth the name and within a minute we stood inside Marks' room, which was scant both in terms of furniture and in its inhabitant's belongings. A bed and wardrobe, small table, small chair and washbasin completed the former while the latter was made up of the contents of two small cases, which lay open upon the floor. Swiftly Holmes lit the oil lamp so that it gave off a dull glow, sufficient for a clandestine search of the premises but with luck insufficient to draw attention to our presence. Eerie shadows flickered unevenly around the small dwelling.

"Stand guard by the door," urged Holmes, already down on the floor and scanning under the bed. I stood, nerves on edge as I awaited the return of the lethal occupant of the room in which we stood, and watched as Holmes methodically rifled the contents of the two cases and searched a suit and bowler hat that hung in the wardrobe. I studied the floor, thankful for the decades of grime and poor cleaning that rendered the old carpet an oily, muddy brown colour. Hopefully this would be sufficient to disguise the evidence of our visit, carrying as we were on our own footwear some of the mud and filth from Blakeney creek. In almost the same time it had taken us to gain access to the room Holmes was done, and I saw him palm away a small card he had found concealed in the lining of the bowler hat. Swiftly he moved to extinguish the lamp, pausing briefly to examine what looked like a tobacco tin on the table, and then we had left the room and were hurrying away down a flight of stairs at the other end of the corridor. During a hurried consultation as we moved away from the King's Arms we agreed to take a trap for the town of Holt, anxious to put some mileage between ourselves and the scene of our recent adventures, but also anxious to challenge the local policeman on the reasons for the stulted investigation into the sinking of the *Misty Jane.*

In the courtyard of the Blakeney Hotel, the largest inn in the village and the fulcrum for the comings and goings to and from the outside world, Holmes and I caught a trap heading for Holt, I suspect one of the last to leave that evening. Holmes confided in me the substance of his discoveries in Marks' room just before we boarded our conveyance.

"I observed a tin of *Players Navy Cut* tobacco by his bedside," muttered Holmes. "Nothing conclusive in that, although it is the same brand that was enjoyed by one of the Sea Marge intruders prior to their entry into Sir Edward's study. Of more interest is this."

He turned over the card he had secreted away from the clothes cupboard. "My assessment is that the bowler hat, along with the suit, comprised his travelling outfit, or was donned whenever business took him away from Blakeney. He clearly acquired this on one of these excursions."

The card was a receipt for a locker storage facility at London's Liverpool Street railway station, the type of facility one might utilise to keep left luggage safe. In my experience such facilities are often employed by wanderers and those with no fixed purpose or accommodation. Indeed, I had used one myself upon washing up in London following my discharge from the army all those years ago.

"With luck we will be able to gain access to the contents of this facility before that beauty even realises the card has disappeared. Nevertheless, we should act swiftly."

Holmes was now deep in thought as we clattered through the dark countryside, but I knew he chafed to conduct an audience with the police in Holt. We eventually disembarked in the town centre of the pretty Georgian town of Holt with the hour approaching six o'clock, and within a few minutes we had located the police station, a redbrick building with a lamp outside. The notice on the door proclaimed that the station closed at six o'clock but my friend and I were in luck. We noticed a light still on inside and on pushing the door it gave, depositing Holmes and myself inside a typical provincial police station.

The man inside, clad in the regulation blue of the village constable, appeared to be about to lock up for the night, and did not seem in the mood to receive visitors. But he started upon recognising Holmes.

"A moment of your time," enjoined Holmes, softly. "I flatter myself that you recognise me. My friend and I are engaged on a case in the district and as part of the wider pattern of the enquiry we are seeking to learn a little more about the sinking of the fishing boat the *Misty Jane* at the mouth of Blakeney channel. We have spoken to the harbour-master who advised us that you, or your good offices, would be preparing a report for the district coroner. Could you assist us? My friend and I are, in all likelihood, only in town for the evening."

Holmes had long possessed the ability to put unwilling helpers at their ease, but I could see that the policeman was irresolute, and seemed, to my mind, desperately ill at ease. For a moment he said nothing. Then he gestured to two chairs that we brought up in front of his desk.

"I should say it is pleasant to meet you both," he began, with the beginnings of a wan smile beginning to make its mark upon his features. "And in other circumstances it would be. But this Blakeney sinking is dogging me like I don't know what."

"Tell me all," replied Holmes smoothly. Our new host, perhaps with one eye on the clock and the advancing hour, gave us a brief summary of all we had hitherto learnt from the two harbour-masters. There was something else though. The brevity of his discussions could not wholly be explained away by encroaching thoughts of his supper. He was guarded and nervous.

"And now," began Holmes in a measured tone, leaning forward and holding the gaze of the policeman, "pray concentrate only on the facts of this case which have given you discomfort."

The policeman initially attempted a puzzled look of innocence, as if to query Holmes' challenge. Then he threw up his hands in surrender.

"It's all so strange and irregular, Mr Holmes. The boat that disappeared off the Dutch coast ... I've no details at all about what happened and nobody seems to be in a position or of a mind to help. On the face of the matter, I've no choice but to support the reaching of a verdict of misadventure. But it's this Blakeney sinking which is really vexing. I've put together what I know after speaking to the coastguard and the port authorities, and there are still a number of questions. I interviewed two witnesses who were golfing on the new course at Cley, half a mile down the coast, and they say they definitely heard an explosion from the area where the *Misty Jane* sank. I had prepared an initial draft report for the coroner and was about to commence trying to discover more about the missing crew when my area superior in Norwich, Detective Superintendent Martin, telephoned me and told me not to pursue the case. Apparently it had been decided at a senior level that in order to avoid further pain to the families of the deceased a simple verdict of accident at sea was to be recorded, and headquarters in Norwich would work with the firm of Mendel & Newcombe in liaising with relatives."

"This is all most irregular and out of process, Mr Holmes. I rang the district coroner's office in Norwich and asked him sceptically if he was happy with a conclusion of 'accident at sea'. I was informed by him that he was, rather uneasily to my mind."

"Are there any other formalities which have to be completed before a case is officially considered closed?" asked Holmes.

The policeman shook his head. "If the coroner's office is satisfied with proceedings, relatives are informed, and no criminal charges are deemed necessary, then the case can be closed. No other government body would be involved. If a larger ship is lost in international waters then a Board of Trade enquiry may be convened, especially if matters of insurance or compensation are involved, but not for a humble fishing boat in inshore waters."

"In any case, something did not ring true on the *Misty Jane* case. I decided to carry on my enquiries in a private capacity, and see if I couldn't discover a little more about these events. I tried to make an appointment to see the coroner personally."

Our policeman now began to look really scared. His voice lowered involuntarily. "I was told the coroner was otherwise engaged and too busy to grant me an interview. Then an army man came to see me. A colonel he was, from Weybourne camp just along the coast. He had three soldiers with him carrying rifles, and they drew up outside here in a big staff car. He told me to leave the *Misty Jane* case. Just that.

Leave it, he said, and close the enquiry. Don't even think about talking to the newspapers. He didn't actually threaten me, but his manner could not have been more menacing if he tried. So that was it. I closed the file, and if, after having spoken to you today, I never hear the name of that boat again, it will still be too soon."

He stood up with an air of finality that told us that as far as he was concerned this conversation, and this eventful chapter in his life, was closed.

"Thank you," said Holmes, as we in turn stood. "What you have told us will remain in our confidence. With any luck you will never have cause to discuss the vessel in question again."

The policeman replied hesitantly. "If you ever find out what all this business is about, I would like to know. If only for the sake of those poor souls who must have died on her ... not to mention the other boat lost off Holland. Be careful though, Mr Holmes. That army man was serious."

Holmes inclined his head and we made our departure. Looking back through the police station window as we moved away, we could see our man gazing forlornly at some papers by light of gas lamp, possibly the early draft of the report he had been so discouraged from completing.

It was now too late to return to Overstrand so we were forced to overnight in Holt, at the Feathers Hotel, a pleasant old coaching inn run by one Cubitt, the proprietor. We obtained a hot meal, made use of the hotel's laundry facilities, and obtained from Cubitt the departure times of trains to Norwich and London the following day.

The adventures of the day and the incredible revelations we had been party to throughout the day had left my companion deep in thought, and myself with a long list of questions that it was clear would remain unanswered this night.

Holmes was terse when I questioned him on recent developments.

"There is a conspiracy brewing, Watson, that much is blatantly clear. These fishing boats were engaged in smuggling, or some other nefarious activity, and their activities clearly have a degree of official connivance. Circumstantial evidence points to the involvement of our own Royal Navy, which also has uncomfortable parallels with the business at Sir Edward's villa. Our trail tomorrow takes us to London, Watson, where I expect a number of leads to mature simultaneously. In addition, sooner or later I will have to meet with Mycroft, particularly concerning the Everard documentation that we are currently holding."

I nodded. "But smuggling what, Holmes? And why from this isolated spot? It seems fairly remote," I added doubtfully.

"On the contrary, Watson, this coastline is perfect. It has isolated creeks with little official oversight or attention. I suspect that this contraband, whatever it may be, is shipped in reasonably small quantities. It is probably sent to the area by rail before being stored at those Holt station sheds we noticed this afternoon, and then delivered at uncertain hours of the night to the secure warehouses we recently surveyed on Blakeney waterfront. The exact nature of the said contraband is still to be revealed. It is clear that the activities of these fellows aroused certain suspicions among the Blakeney locals, however. In the various testimonies we have heard today, a number of incongruities have emerged between the activities of these gentlemen and the normal conduct of ordinary fishermen."

"And how in Heaven's name do these recent developments relate to the activities of the Everard, Haag and Massner community?" I asked, exasperated.

"Not now, Watson, or we could be discussing the matter half the night! We can talk further in due course. Now I intend to get some rest, and formulate a plan for the 'morrow."

Holmes had impressed upon me the absolute need for an early start the next day, so I also turned in, eagerly awaiting the next day's developments.

Chapter Seven

Conspiracy in the Capital?

True to his word, Holmes roused me before dawn with a knock on my door and, after a snatched breakfast, we walked swiftly to Holt railway station to catch an early train to Norwich and London via Cromer. At the station my friend gazed intently in the first light of day at the storage facilities and outbuildings surrounding the tracks, and then nodded and grunted to himself, as if contented that his working hypothesis was supported by his recent observations. During the uneventful journey to London Holmes outlined his plan for our activities in the capital.

"As I mentioned yesterday, it is important that the contents of the deposit locker at Liverpool Street be inspected quickly. With luck Marks will not have noticed the absence of the ticket in the past twenty-four hours, especially if we managed to successfully cover our tracks following the illicit search of his room. The left luggage office at Liverpool Street station shall be our first port of call, followed by a clandestine inspection of the contents of Marks' locker. Following that … I believe we should divide. You make your way to the offices of

Wiggins in the East End of London and see if he has anything of interest to tell us with regards to the missing items from Sir Edward's London property. He will recognise you from our times together and will take you into his confidence. After that, if you will be so kind, perhaps you could make your way to the photographic specialist in New Oxford Street ... I will supply you with the address ... and recover the photograph I borrowed from Sir Edward's offices in High Holborn, together with any inflated reproductions that Mr Radley may have been able to produce for us. With luck the details of our man's clothing or uniform should be revealed, which in turn may leave us opportunity for further enquiries into his background and identity via the Regimental Sergeant-Major of his regiment."

"If this proves to be the case, as a former army man yourself, you may be able to begin advancing this next stage of the enquiry in my absence. There may be nothing to the mysterious Mr Caulfield who left the employ of Sir Edward so suddenly, but did you note the reference in Blakeney yesterday to a Mr Naylor who represents Mendel & Newcombe? Cook clearly stated he had a large red birthmark upon his features, as does the gentleman whose photograph currently resides with our London specialist. Such occurrences are perhaps rare enough to warrant our bearing the coincidence in mind. In any case, I recommend we reconvene for a late afternoon tea at your rooms in Queen Anne Street."

"Very well, Holmes. Where will you be?"

"I have a number of visits I am required to make," replied my friend, as the train continued steadily on its journey towards London. "Among other things, I am going to make it my business to discover a few more facts concerning the mysterious firm of Mendel & Newcombe," he muttered darkly.

In line with Holmes' recent discourses my colleague and I disembarked at Liverpool Street station and made our way quickly to the left luggage locker area. As the morning was by now well advanced the station was quieter than might otherwise have been the case, and the left luggage area particularly, being situated in an alcove in a little–traversed section of the station, was virtually deserted.

"Collect the item," urged Holmes, handing me the ticket and moving to a position out of the vision of the ticket clerk. Puzzled, I handed the Blakeney ticket to the left luggage man and received a parcel in return some twelve inches by eight inches. It was a heavy packet well bound in brown paper and secured with string. It was the work of a few moments to find a nook away from prying eyes, whereupon I produced a penknife and freed the package of its brown paper – several layers – and retaining string. A cardboard box with lid lay beneath. On lifting the lid we immediately saw the flash of dark gunmetal and I reached in and withdrew a handgun, not a revolver but a Webley & Scott self-loading pistol. I peered at the weapon. My interest in firearms was to hold me in good stead.

"This is a new model," I whispered to Holmes, "and a new design, I believe. They are currently coming into service with our Royal Navy and Royal Marines."

"Are they now?" mused Holmes rhetorically. Other contents of the box included compact nautical charts of the Dutch coast around Rotterdam and The Hague; a map of the London Docks area from the Pool of London to Limehouse; a wad of English pound notes; some rounds for the pistol, and what looked like a small white business card. The words

'Whitehall 821' were typed in flowing black script across the card. Holmes studied the card intently and gave me a look I could not read.

"What does it all mean, Holmes? And what do we do with all these items?"

"It means that these items are very dear to the current occupant of room number four at The King's Arms, Blakeney," intoned my companion, "who took precautions to ensure that they were viewed by no-one but himself. These items represent further evidence for our naval conspiracy. The charts are most revealing. It was implied that the *Yarmouth Adventuress* was lost off the Dutch coast, was it not? And these maps of the London docks. Most singular … the base for further mysterious waterborne activity, perhaps? As for the goods themselves, since we cannot return them whence they came in a condition which suggests they have not been researched, let us return them in the box to the locker and be rid of them. Mr Marks can have no proof it was us who intercepted these items, even if he may have his strong suspicions."

"What about the attendant, Holmes?"

Holmes shrugged. "A number of people leave items here all the time, and the luggage clerks must deal with dozens of enquiries per day. You will remember I asked you to collect the item, and will ask you to return it. I flatter myself that an attendant would find it easier to recall the face of Mr Sherlock Holmes than that of Dr John Watson. I think" – here Holmes took another long look at the chart and map – "that these have told us all that they can. All except this!" He looked at the small business card again thoughtfully, then slipped it away into his waistcoat.

"Come Watson, return this box and let us go about our separate business as agreed. We will rendezvous at your rooms at four o'clock."

With that Holmes strode away in the direction of the Underground system.

For my part, having returned the box into the keeping of the left luggage attendant, I headed down towards the East End of London, down those cobbled streets and alleyways, and navigated the narrow lanes where market stalls were laid out and vendors proclaimed their wares. In no time at all I had located the offices of Wiggins and prepared to re-acquaint myself with him after all this time.

Wiggins looked serious as I entered his office, and he greeted me coolly with a set face. I looked at him curiously.

"My people have located those missing items, Dr Watson. Some of them at least. The silver we found being handled by a known silver fence near Bow. One of my people used to move in those circles and, as a favour, got a look at the goblets as they were being hammered ready for melting down. Flat as pancakes they were, Dr Watson, but the hallmark serial numbers matched those on the list Mr Holmes gave me. One of the pictures turned up in a grubby pawnbrokers just off Aldgate. I tell you all this in confidence, mind, Dr Watson ... no police. This was a favour and I had to give my word there would be no police involved. Especially now," he said, almost accusingly.

"Very well," I acquiesced, unsure as to whether as I was agreeing to something I could not honour. Wiggins seemed to be agitated about something, but I chose to press on and wait for him to come out with it.

"Did your ... people get a description of the persons who supplied these items to these ... outlets?" I asked.

"Mr Holmes didn't ask that," muttered Wiggins. "I guess I could take you to the pawnbroker, at least. The other contacts of mine won't see you, Dr Watson, begging your pardon. But see here, Dr Watson, there's more. Old Gunther Haag was killed yesterday."

"What!" I cried, half rising from my chair.

Wiggins went on hurriedly. "Shot dead by police. They came to take him for questioning but he was killed in the scuffle. Friend of mine on the local paper got the story. He reckoned they were special police because the ordinary coppers don't go armed. There's still police there now. I trust Mr Holmes, but I couldn't help feeling that all this had something to do with his visit the other day. Even if he was a German, he had never done any of us any harm. People round here look after their own and there's a lot of resentment against what happened to Gunther."

I chose my next words carefully. "I have known Mr Holmes for thirty years and in all that time he has never wittingly betrayed a confidence or acted without the highest of moral intentions. If this is indeed indirectly due to your assistance of the past few days, rest assured that Mr Holmes would not have planned it that way. Also, as you know, Mr Holmes has always been a private investigator and affiliated to no official agency."

Privately my mind was reeling. However Haag had come to forfeit his life, it seemed inescapable that only Mycroft could have precipitated the actions that ultimately lead to his death.

Wiggins nodded. "I accept all that. But you'll forgive me if I lie low after taking you to this pawnbroker. I don't need the damage to my name and business from helping detectives, begging your pardon, Dr Watson, even if you ain't *official*."

I spread my hands and nodded.

Moments later Wiggins had donned cap and coat and we were threading our way through the streets of the East End towards Aldgate. On the way Wiggins went out of his way to take me past Haag's store. One window was boarded up and a policeman stood on guard outside the premises. Wiggins caught my eye as we passed and nodded at the place surreptitiously.

"A couple of local people heard gunfire," he commented after we had passed. I nodded grimly. "How many shots were fired?" I asked, not really expecting this degree of detail.

"Three," replied Wiggins, who smiled at me sheepishly on registering my surprise.

"I have a lot of contacts in this part of London," he said, "who are privy to a great deal of information." He gave me a wink and I did not press the issue further.

Before long we reached the pawnbroker's shop in question, a grimy, dilapidated building with the belongings of the desperate arrayed dispassionately in the window. We passed into the gloomy interior and Wiggins introduced me to the proprietor, an unsavoury, stooped individual who regarded me dolefully from behind a counter almost buried under every type of personal belonging from old jewellery to pipes and books.

Mr Haster, the proprietor, seemed most anxious to impress upon me his innocence, and that of his business, in the eyes of the law. It seemed to me, however, that Mr Haster was not the type of man to be too discerning, or the type to ask too many questions, as to the provenance of items which came into his care. In any event, I was forced to avow my separation from any official authority, and to declare the content of our conversations confidential, before Haster agreed to speak to me in detail. Wiggins sat in a covered chair that had received the attentions of several moths while Haster and I spoke.

"The piece you are interested in is this," said Haster. "It is a very minor work by a near unknown artist. I would not normally have taken it, but the artist was a contemporary of Turner's, and may be worth something if only through association."

I looked at the piece, a typical English pastoral scene, simply framed. It did indeed, to my untrained eye, seem unremarkable.

"What of the persons who left it here?" I asked.

"There was only one man. He came and left in a frantic hurry. A big, heavy man, with a mop of straw-coloured hair, and a distinctive red flash covering part of his face. A birthmark, or particular injury, I would expect."

"Indeed?" I queried, trying to control my excitement. "Where exactly was this mark?" I asked, conscious of my visit to Holmes' photographic man later in the afternoon.

The pawnbroker thought hard. "Just below his right eye and stretching down his cheek and to the bridge of his nose."

"You seem very sure?" I fixed the man with a level gaze.

The pawnbroker returned my gaze calmly. "In my line of work I deal with all types of people, from the upstanding and trustworthy to the less so. The ability to memorise facial features is a knack I have acquired, you might say."

"I accept that," I replied. "Thank you for your assistance. I may have to recover that picture from you. I would ask that you hold it for me for two weeks, and if I come for it I will ensure the correct payment is made. Be rid of it in that time, and I will count my previous confidentiality agreement redundant and have no hesitation in speaking to the authorities on your status as a receiver of stolen goods. Is it agreed?"

"And if red-flash comes for it in the meantime?"

"Do not release it. Say you are having the piece independently valued, or similar, and arrange a time at a later date when he can collect it. And then inform me."

I handed him my business card. He nodded, glancing up at me darkly. Wiggins nodded to him and we both left the shop.

"Did you get what you were after, Dr Watson?" Wiggins asked me.

"I think I may have done," I smiled. "Time will tell."

"A nasty piece of work, he is, Dr Watson. You dealt with him nicely."

"And what of you and your business?" I replied. "He seemed like a man who could hold a grudge. Will he not use your co-operation with me against you?"

"Not that one," laughed Wiggins. "I've got too much against him and his past activities!"

Shortly afterwards Wiggins and I parted with the promise that Holmes and I would contact him again in the future when the situation was quieter. I then moved swiftly across London in pursuit of my second appointment of the day, at the photographic specialist's premises on New Oxford Street. Mr Radley, the specialist, seemed ready enough to deal with me when I presented him with the receipt for his services that Holmes had given me.

"One moment, Dr Watson," he said, as he disappeared into his dark room at the rear of his shop. The science of photography was still very much in development and I stared around his shop with considerable professional curiosity. Glass photographic plates, cameras, leather cases and all the photographic paraphernalia of the day were very much in evidence.

In no time at all Radley had returned bearing two envelopes. The first, I was informed, held the original photograph Holmes had borrowed from Sir Edward's Holborn offices. The second, a more substantial envelope, carried two enlarged copies of the photograph in question. Even as I paid the man my curiosity got the better of me and I opened the second envelope, extracting one of the enlargements. The face that stared back at me was a burly one with a great shock of hair. What was more, a birthmark covered a large part of the right hand side of his face, beginning just under his eye, stretching down his cheek and just touching the centre of the bridge of his nose. I exhaled heavily. The pawnbroker's description matched this fellow identically. I looked again at the magnified details of the fellow's dress, and saw the button that had caught Holmes' attention. A crest was in evidence on the button, but it was not an army crest, as Holmes had at first supposed. I bit my lip as I viewed the anchor emblem of the army's sister service, the Royal Navy. Moreover, as I scrutinised the features of his uniform more intently, it became clear that the fellow was not a ranker.

"Officer, Royal Navy," I muttered to the bemused photographer, giving voice to my thoughts.

I took my leave of Radley and hurried off in a state of anticipation towards Queen Anne Street to make my afternoon *rendezvous* with Holmes. With my pocket watch showing five minutes to four, I rounded the corner of Queen Anne Street and walked quickly towards my lodgings. Sure enough, approaching my rooms from the other direction but making similarly good time, was Holmes. There were a number of people on the street but Holmes caught sight of me through the crowd and waved at me. We both converged on my rooms and had almost reached the door when we both happened to glance across the street, where a newspaper boy was manning a stall and advertising *The Evening Standard* in typically vocal style.

"Foreign Office Man killed at home!" he shouted lustily. "Shooting at Swiss Cottage!"

Holmes was across the street quicker than I and within moments we were both poring over the afternoon edition of the newspaper in my withdrawing room. The lead story told of how senior Foreign Office translator Felix Massner had been found dead from gunshot wounds in his Swiss Cottage home. A concerned neighbour had apparently called the police after hearing the shots, which had occurred late last night. The police investigating the death were not offering suicide as a possibility, although no possible motives or reasons for the killing were stated.

"But, Holmes," I stammered, "Gunther Haag was also shot dead yesterday, at his shop."

"Ah," replied Holmes, looking at me evenly. He stood and walked to the window, where he stood with his back to me for several moments. Finally he turned, his face grim. "It appears the principals of this plot are concluding their business rather effectively. It is to be hoped that we, too, do not feature any more dramatically in this business than has been the case to date," he said, dryly. "Pray, tell me all."

Swiftly I outlined my discoveries of the day to my companion, beginning with the news of Gunther Haag's untimely demise. I went on to describe my findings at the pawnbrokers premises and at the photographic specialists.

At the conclusion of my monologue Holmes was silent for a few moments before replying. He looked heavy-hearted.

"As you have no doubt concluded, both Massner and Haag have met their deaths after I put Mycroft on to them. The time has come for an interview with my brother. As for our Mr Naylor, he and this shady London operative, Mr Caulfield, would appear to be one and the same," commented Holmes. "Now you have revealed his Navy connections, and the fact that he was an officer, I can approach a contact of mine in Devon and see if we can't learn a little more about our mysterious subject."

"Devon?" I queried.

"The long-time commandant of the Royal Naval College, Dartmouth," replied Holmes. "I was once able to assist him in extricating himself from a small financial scandal, in which he was entirely innocent, but which threatened to ruin him. All Naval officer cadets pass out from Dartmouth. Armed even with the limited information we have, and given the peculiar affliction affecting Naylor's face, we should be able to discover something further in short order. I will send my contact a telegram from your local Post Office now. I will also telephone Mycroft's office and attempt to arrange an interview for tomorrow."

I could tell that my friend was somewhat distracted by the news of the sudden demise of Haag and Massner.

"How was your day?" I asked, in an effort to disrupt his thoughts.

After a moment's reflection Holmes replied.

"I spent a most informative day at Companies House, and then at the Lloyd's building with its *Register of British and Foreign Shipping*. The firm of Mendel & Newcombe is distinctly singular, Watson. It exists on paper, indeed so, but its registered address is a Post Office box number. It is nigh on untraceable without some supporting information. I went to the address that our mysterious Mr Naylor had given the harbour-master of Blakeney, Cook, as a business address for Mendel & Newcombe ... number 30, Brushfield Street. This is a fictitious address, Watson. Brushfield Street exists, opposite Spitalfields market, but there is no number 30. I spoke to an attendant manning a reception desk in the office next door. He advised me that he occasionally takes delivery of mail for Mendel & Newcombe but immediately forwards it on to the same Post Office box number I found listed at Companies House. Apparently the arrangement is of long-standing. The man I spoke to was clearly an innocent and he, and his colleagues, obviously believe themselves to be merely rectifying a clerical error of some kind."

"And the fishing vessels?"

"They *are* registered to Mendel & Newcombe. All three of our acquaintance; the *Misty Jane,* the *Yarmouth Adventuress,* and the *Pearl.* I discovered that the firm own another marine asset, a small freighter named the *Lindisfarne,* which is berthed in the London docks area, and have taken a contract on a small warehouse that abuts her moorings. It is my intention that we mount a discreet reconnaissance of this vessel under cover of darkness this evening."

"Another clandestine operation, Holmes?"

Holmes held up a hand. "Possibly. It is fair to assume that the *Lindisfarne* is engaged in similar activities as her counterparts in Blakeney. We may learn more this evening. However, now I must despatch a telegram to Dartmouth, and make a telephone call to Mycroft's office. I will also speak to Sir Edward Muster on the telephone while I am about it."

Holmes was gone almost an hour and it was dark by the time he returned.

"It is done," he said. "I have sent my missive to Dartmouth with the request for an exceedingly rapid reply. We have an interview with Mycroft tomorrow at a government office at eleven o'clock sharp. I told him that we have a package for him, recovered from Sir Daniel Everard's home in Overstrand. As I suspected, he is so eager to lay his hands on the contents of same that he seemed quite ready to overlook our little transgression in removing the item. I said that in return we had quite a number of questions on which we would be seeking clarity," Holmes muttered coldly.

"Oh, and I spoke to Sir Edward Muster," my friend added almost as an afterthought.

"What news from Overstrand?" I queried.

"As we anticipated, Sir Daniel's body was discovered by the maid when she attended work this morning. I understand that the death is not being viewed as suspicious by the local constabulary, although in view of his standing, I would be surprised if a post-mortem examination were not carried out in due course. Sir Edward told me that Chief Inspector Carlisle's Special Branch detail had left his property, and had now turned their attentions to The Gables, Sir Daniel's place. It seems evident that the establishment have already made the appropriate connections following their researches in the premises of Haag and Massner, respectively."

"All the more reason to see Mycroft, then, Holmes, and hand over these documents."

Holmes merely nodded. "Sir Edward told me that he had been informed by Carlisle, in confidence, that Sir Daniel was part of a German spy ring and had been behind the attempts on his properties. The story that Carlisle told was that

Everard's German handlers wanted to discover the state of Sir Edward's connections with the British Government. He then swore Sir Edward to secrecy on the grounds that what had occurred in Overstrand and Belgravia over the last few days was directly related to matters of national security. Sir Edward said that he was told that he could reveal these details to his wife and closest confidantes, but to no one else on pain of penalty. Sir Edward was also of the impression that, as we suspected, there was a desire to keep Everard's treachery secret on account of his social position."

"What did you say to Sir Edward?"

Holmes reflected for a moment, and took a deep breath.

"I told him that, in my opinion he had unwittingly been at the mercy of dark forces in recent days, but that now the storm had passed. I advised him to try to clear these events from his mind and continue with his life and career. I told him that I believed that he and his family and household were now safe; but that if he was ever of any apprehension that this was not the case, he only had to call upon me and I would come at once. I said that I do not usually leave a case in such a mysterious manner, but that my hand had been forced by a number of unforeseen events which made the events at Sea Marge appear only the eye in a very complex storm. He seemed relieved at my reassurances and advised me he would send our luggage back to us care of your address. I further stated that we could arrange the return to him of one of the pieces of art stolen from his London residence, but that I feared that the other items were lost forever. He gave me a degree of thanks I did not feel I had really earned, and the conversation ended. I do not believe he will seek any further clarity on recent events, subject as he is to a binding national security stricture."

There was silence but for the ticking of the grandfather clock in the hall.

"Where does this business leave us, Holmes? What to make of it? We have dealt with a number of very disparate events in this business, and seem no farther forward, at least as far as poor Sir Edward is concerned."

"I suspect all will become clear tomorrow," muttered Holmes darkly. "I believe I understand the situation of recent days and weeks, but I shall need to interview Mycroft. Come, let us partake of some supper and then prepare for our survey of the *Lindisfarne* on the river."

After supper, at approximately eight o'clock in the evening, Holmes and I donned warm overcoats and scarves and, as seemed to have been the policy on this particular adventure, again pocketed our revolvers. In addition I took up a stout oak walking stick that was propped up just beneath my coat-stand in the hall. Holmes led as we ventured out into the cold evening air, the chill promising frost and a half-moon offering light from above. We chose not to take any transport and headed on foot in the direction of St Paul's cathedral. Before long we saw that great edifice towering above us, gleaming white in the evening air, whereupon we turned and started to move downhill, towards the river and the wharves and quays of the greatest port in the world.

As we moved off the main arteries and thoroughfares of the City so the number of persons out and about became fewer and fewer. The black oil and gas lamps seemed also to grow fewer, until the odd one that still illuminated our walk seemed to throw flickering, malevolent shadows across the very cobbles and pavements upon which we walked. The only sound I seemed to hear was that of our footsteps as we moved ever closer towards the river. We crossed Upper or maybe Lower Thames Street – I forget which – and before long turned right down a narrow alley, overlooked by towering Victorian warehouses. Fully six stories high, a number of walkways crossed between the buildings at all levels above our heads, installed to facilitate the movement of goods away from the riverside and into these great storage houses for sorting, packaging, and onward despatch. In daylight, with stevedores, packers, and dockworkers going about their business this area would be a hive of activity. Now, with the onset of night, the place was deserted, and with a mist creeping in off the Thames these sinister brick edifices seemed to crowd in upon us, crushing us and assailing our spirits.

At the end of the alley Holmes and I suddenly found ourselves near the waterfront, and a glimmer of light was provided not only by the moon above but also from the twinkling of lights from across the river. The river could not have been more than sixty feet from us, yet our onward passage was barred by a set of iron gates, secured by chains and padlocks. Peering through the railings I could recognise the outlines of a small steamer ahead and to the left, moored up against a quay. At least I could believe she was small in the world of international shipping, but on that atmospheric evening, with the imagination playing havoc with the mind, she seemed colossal, her main funnel and bridge rearing up above us and the name, '*Lindisfarne, London*', emblazoned upon her stern. She was definitely a freighter. Holmes had withdrawn night glasses from within the folds of his clothing and was gazing intently at her bridge, where even I could discern two lights, such as those provided by the cigarettes of two men smoking companionably side by side. There was near silence but for the background hum of the great river, and even though the men were no real distance from me I could not hear what, if anything, these two men were saying.

Holmes stared through his scope for some time before snapping it shut and moving back down the alley. I followed him, hoping that our night's adventure might soon be over, but he darted down a passage running off the alley that I had not spotted, and we came out behind a warehouse. Shrouded in darkness we edged around the rear and up the side of the building until we once more faced the river. We advanced forward towards the waterfront and peered around the left hand front edge of the building. A vicious barbed wire fence again barred our path from the area of wharf and unloading space directly in front of the freighter, but in the time it had taken us to skirt the building, two men – presumably the ones we had initially observed – had alighted on the quay and were conversing not forty feet from where we stood. Again I could not make out the conversation, but it was impossible not to recognise the Navy issue mufti in which the men were attired. Holmes also seemed to have noted this. He tapped my shoulder and we stealthily withdrew back along the side of the warehouse.

As we retreated I saw one small window only which had not been boarded up and secured and Holmes cupped his eyes and looked inside for a full thirty seconds. I nervously scanned the dockside area around me, anticipating a repeat of the Blakeney incident with, perhaps, far more serious consequences. To the left a new set of wharves and quays were visible, the preserve of iron and coal merchants boasting brick and timber storage facilities. Seeing Holmes peering so intently into the warehouse sparked my curiosity, however, and I pressed my face up against the window in a similar manner. I could not see much, aided as I was only by the light of the moon, but I could just discern a number of packing crates, Government issue by their appearance. Just as I was about to turn away, however, I caught sight of the unmistakeable silhouette of a rifle leaning against the inside wall of the warehouse. I realised that Holmes had also seen what I had. I immediately wondered whether the weapon belonged to one of the crew, or whether it was a sample from a larger consignment currently residing in those mysterious crates. In either event, the discovery raised yet further questions as to the nature and operations of Mendel & Newcombe.

Eventually my companion and I moved off and we walked quickly but as quietly as we could back up the alley and away from the docks area. In hushed whispers, once away from the scene of our recent discoveries, Holmes and I compared notes on what we had seen. As we walked, the quiet that had accompanied us ever since we approached the docks basin remained, but to my fevered mind I seemed to hear the sound of footsteps other than our own, following us in the murk and the gloom.

"Holmes," I whispered without breaking stride, "I think we are being followed."

"You are accurate in your thinking, Watson," said Holmes evenly. "We are but moments from the tram routes near St Paul's and should be able to lose our unwelcome shadow there."

My friend quickened his pace and as the great clock struck ten o'clock we boarded a night tram back towards the West End and, one hoped, safety. As we pulled away I could have sworn I saw a figure in a dark outfit, not fifty feet away, regarding our conveyance from an alley parallel to the one from which we had just emerged. Soon we had pulled away and he was lost in the shadows and the gloom.

"Well, Watson," said my friend as we travelled. "Curiouser and curiouser," he commented enigmatically.

Chapter Eight

Dénouement

The following morning Holmes received a telegram which he opened and scanned quickly as we sat at breakfast.

"From Dartmouth," he grunted. "The information I was seeking."

Leaving me to deal with the implications of this statement, and offering no further explanation, Holmes uttered not another word over breakfast. He was similarly subdued as the morning progressed. Eventually, at a quarter past ten, Holmes rose from his chair in the withdrawing room, where he had been studying the events surrounding the demise of Felix Massner in the morning newspapers. He checked his pocket watch assiduously, and withdrew from his waistcoat a small business card that he studied thoughtfully.

"Come Watson," he said, "let us walk. It promises to be a most pleasant day." Holmes spoke lightly, but his face was set.

I sensed that, whatever the contents of the interview that Holmes had arranged for the morning, the *dénouement* of our adventure was upon us. My friend picked up the documents we had liberated from Sir Daniel Everard's property and moved towards the front door. Donning my greatcoat I followed my friend out into the street and we walked down onto Regent Street. The sun was shining in a cloudless sky and the metropolis was swarming with workers going about their daily business. Turning right at Piccadilly Circus we carried on down Piccadilly, with Holmes walking purposefully at speed, and then crossed the park to come into the district of St. James'. Holmes crossed Birdcage Walk and unerringly found a gap between the splendid town houses lining the pavement, which brought us out into the elegant surroundings of Queen Anne's Gate. No stranger to London, nevertheless I had had few occasions to enter this imperious courtyard, a stone's throw from Westminster and in the very heart of Establishment London. Regal Georgian townhouses, with full length draped windows, made up the accommodation around the square. The red brick was offset by black iron railings and austere black streetlamps at pavement level. Possessing only the knowledge of British politics that any reader of *The Times* could demonstrate, still I knew that within this mews dwelt a veritable pantheon of Whitehall notables, including the veteran politician Lord Haldane and Lord Fisher, Mr Churchill's predecessor as First Sea Lord.

"Is this where you had your first interview with Mycroft last week?" I asked as we walked. Holmes shook his head in the negative.

"These here are his private offices. The address corresponds to the one listed on this highly exclusive business card he gave me at the outset of the adventure." Holmes flashed the small business card at me that he had been fingering earlier that morning.

I was forced to hurry as Holmes walked straight up to a black door on the far side of the square and knocked loudly. Within a few seconds the door was opened by an immaculately dressed doorman and, clearly without the need to show our credentials, we were shown through an anteroom and into a large study towards the back of the house. Fine art lined the walls in both rooms and the low wooden beams were warmly offset by terracotta wallpaper. Despite the comparative warmth of the day a fire was burning in an enormous hearth. These details I recalled only later, as a succession of minor shocks at the identity of the room's occupants initially drove them from my mind. The room was thick with smoke, not only from the blaze but also from a number of cigars that the aforementioned occupants of the room were smoking.

Standing upright next to a large wooden writers desk that dominated the room was a young man of commanding presence whom I recognised immediately. First Lord of the Admiralty Winston Churchill was dressed in a narrow pinstripe suit and smoking one of his trademark King Edward cigars; he held a sheaf of reports in his left hand. He nodded to us briefly. Seated away from the desk to the right sat a middle-aged man in full naval uniform whose tunic was festooned with decorations for valour. He had the look of a man I felt I should recognise but could not place. In addition to these two, a third man sat in a high-backed swivel chair behind the desk, plumes of cigar smoke spiralling above him, but as the chair back was facing us, I could not make him out.

If my companion was taken aback by the esteemed company in which we found ourselves, he did not show it; on the contrary, he seemed perfectly composed.

"Gentlemen!" he cried, striding forward and hurling the business card he had produced that morning onto the desk, "let me return your business card. 'Number 12 Queen Anne's Gate, London SW' it says thereon. My companion and I have an appointment here at eleven o'clock sharp, and by my pocket watch we are punctual."

"Indeed you are, Sherlock," came a deep voice I recognised from behind the director's chair. It swung round slowly and I found myself face to face with Mycroft Holmes.

"Please sit, gentlemen."

"Mycroft," I stammered involuntarily. I was surprised not at seeing him here in Westminster, which, even though he was supposedly retired, was his natural *milieu,* but at his inclusion in such an elite and enigmatic trio.

"It is good to see you again, Doctor," he smiled. "Let me introduce my associates. Mr Churchill, the First Lord of the Admiralty, I believe you will both recognise. The gentleman to my left is Captain Mansfield Cumming, the head of Department Six of Military Intelligence. You will never see his name, occupation and career details in print anywhere during your lifetime. I would ask you both to respect his anonymity and keep the details of this interview strictly secret."

Mycroft smiled at me again. "You perhaps little thought when I asked Sherlock and yourself to look into a raid on a country mansion that it would develop into a hunt for one of the most dangerous German spy rings on these shores."

I acquiesced that this was so.

"I too found this development interesting," said Sherlock coldly, "especially in light of the fact that you chose to withhold all manner of vital information from Watson and I at the outset of our investigation. It also sits ill with me that, having confided in you some suspicions I had with regards to the activities of certain individuals, the next I hear of the individuals in question is that they are both shot dead in unclear, nay mysterious, circumstances!"

While this exchange was taking place, coffee was served in fine chinaware.

Mycroft regarded his brother dispassionately. His jaw was set. "*Vital information* ... Sherlock?" enquired Mycroft airily, echoing Holmes' previous comment, and seemingly offering a challenge for elucidation.

"Oh, tssk!" said Sherlock irritably. "Sir Edward Muster never was in any danger, was he? At least, not from any German agencies or individuals, which you intimated to me could have been the case at the very outset of this investigation. Chief Inspector Carlisle's Special Branch men were not present in Norfolk as investigating detectives, or as armed protection; they were there as surveillance operatives who conducted a discreet survey of Sea Marge, especially Sir Edward's study and any other repositories of interesting documentation, and at the same time kept a watch on him, his household, and, I suspect, all his communications. During the whole course of this business you had Sir Edward under virtual house arrest, although he did not recognise it as such. In addition, the illicit entries into his properties last week were carried out by specialist military personnel acting under the orders of yourself and, presumably, the other men in this room."

Holmes turned to me.

"I said to you Watson, did I not, when you asked me why I chose to begin the investigation in Norfolk rather than in London, that I had an idea ... that the Norfolk raid bore the hallmarks of men who knew what they were looking for. I was correct. The men *did* know what they were looking for;

namely documents and information giving details of Sir Edward's business, political and social connections and recent activities, and they began their search in that room where many a secret is to be found, namely, the study. The men in question did not have time to complete their search, however, before they were disturbed by Mr Wilson, Sir Edward's business manager, and were forced to flee the premises. However, this bumbling adventure gave the pretext for Special Branch men to occupy the house, again under your direction, Mycroft, and make their own discreet assessment of the contents of Sir Edward's study. The Belgravia operation, carried out at the same time, had the same aim in mind ... namely the assessment of Sir Edward's personal, business, and political affairs ... although the affair was clumsily carried out to give the illusion that knowledgeable professional thieves were at work, and a few small items were removed to give substance to the lie."

I looked at Mr Churchill and Captain Cumming. Mr Churchill was now seated, and both he and the naval man maintained a stony silence.

I looked over at Holmes. "But what of Inspector Jackson, whom we first met at Sea Marge? He seemed most genial and earnest. I cannot believe he was involved in this ... duplicity?" I asked my friend.

"Inspector Jackson and his team were not involved," replied Holmes, holding to Mycroft's level gaze. "When we first arrived at Sea Marge he had got down to business in a most competent manner, and was, as far as he knew, pursuing a legitimate enquiry. Clearly having such a competent Special Branch detective launch what appeared to be a serious investigation into the night-time events at Sea Marge at the outset, helped create and maintain the illusion that the British authorities were determined to get to the bottom of the matter, and were solicitous for Sir Edward's welfare. You will remember, however, Watson, that after a few days Jackson was recalled to London and replaced by the overbearing Chief Inspector Carlisle, whose men, all bearing the unmistakeable stamp of former military personnel, began to pursue a very different agenda at Sea Marge."

I stared at Holmes, amazed. "Was such an ... operation ... duplicated at Halkin Place?"

"There was no need," replied Holmes, still staring coolly at Mycroft. "Halkin Place was comprehensively searched from top to bottom. Mycroft's agents had no further business there. The Metropolitan Police who carried out the investigation in Belgravia were, like Jackson, doing so legitimately, but I suspect they will draw a blank as to the perpetrators, and their official findings will be inconclusive."

"This is all most interesting, Sherlock," commented Mycroft, non-committally.

Holmes put his hands on Mycroft's desk and leaned towards him so that his face was merely inches from his brother's. "So, Sir Edward was under suspicion for espionage, or treason, against the State. You had his residential properties covered, and you had inserted one of your people into his business earlier in the year under the guise of a bicycle courier. The timing of this made me think your interest in Sir Edward may have been related to his activities at the International Opium Conference in The Hague, of December last year and January this, at which, I understand, Sir Edward adopted a very controversial position."

Holmes now rose, and began striding in short lengths up and down the small study.

"Sir Edward was under suspicion of activities directly affecting British national security. And yet during my time in Overstrand I established the identity of the real spy for the Germans, notably Sir Daniel Everard, and provided *you* with the information that you were to employ for the destruction of the ring of which he was a member."

Holmes paused as he looked at Mycroft once more. "I confess I am ... taken aback at the methods employed to effect the removal of this threat to these islands. The newspapers have graphically covered the events in Swiss Cottage and in the Bethnal Green Road. I suspect there will be a police enquiry into the death of old Gunther Haag, but no doubt you and your office will deflect it behind the scenes, and I would not be at all surprised if the assassins of Felix Massner are never brought to justice, and the case remains ... unsolved ... shall we say."

Mycroft stared back at Holmes, unblinking. His companions were similarly silent. Holmes resumed his pacing up and down the study as his revelations continued.

"You may ask how I placed you and your associates at the heart of things, and identified you as the puppet-master," Holmes stated. He continued. "Sir Daniel's last report to his contact, Massner, contained a reference to two fishing vessels that you, Mr Churchill, have used in the past to ferry yourself and your party from an Admiralty warship to the beach at Overstrand, from whence you would walk up to your holiday cottage in the village. No doubt this was a mere whim on your part, but this reference became significant when I learnt of the mysterious loss of both these vessels within a day of one another. As you know, Mycroft, I do not like coincidences and there were some very singular facts surrounding both boats. Both were owned by the mysterious firm of Mendel &

Newcombe. Both were lost in unusual circumstances; the *Yarmouth Adventuress* seemingly disappeared without trace somewhere off the Dutch coast, and the *Misty Jane* supposedly suffered a fire at the approach to Blakeney estuary. Through collusion with the local coastguard I examined the wreckage of the latter and found clear evidence of an explosion. As a chemist of some note, and armed with some specialist knowledge, I was able to establish that she had been sunk by a charge of dynamite, or another explosive of some kind. Moreover, it soon became clear that the enquiries into the disappearance of the two vessels were being obstructed by directives issued at a senior level."

"Only yesterday I spent a most illuminating afternoon at Companies House and the Lloyd's building, home to the national register of shipping for both British and foreign vessels. At the former I researched the provenance of the firm of Mendel & Newcombe and discovered some interesting facts. Only formed in the autumn of last year, this company currently boasts four sea-going assets; three Norfolk fishing boats and a small freighter named the *Lindisfarne*. Only, in flagrant breach of British company law, there was no address listed for a company headquarters, merely a distinctly suspicious Post Office box number. Perhaps you would care to confirm the Post Office box number in question, Mycroft? I ask *you* this only because I found *your* name among the list of directors!"

I looked at Holmes, then Mycroft, incredulously. Mycroft's features did not register a flicker of emotion. Utter silence prevailed in the room. Holmes carried on relentlessly, holding to his brother's stony gaze.

"At Lloyd's I could not advance my knowledge of the history of your fishing vessels, as they were not significant enough to merit inclusion in the official records. But the *Lindisfarne*, as a merchantman exceeding one thousand gross tonnes, was indeed recorded, together with her history and current whereabouts. A colourful history, Mycroft. At one stage in her career I found she had been owned by the Admiralty and had been fitted out as a minesweeper. Some exotic locations on her past port roster too, notably in the Middle East and Asia. Perhaps she has been used to run arms, or similar clandestine cargo, into areas of the world where the British Empire is reluctant to be seen to be meddling directly? Eh, Mycroft?" Holmes laughed harshly. "I don't think I am far wide of the mark."

"I found her current location to be at a quiet wharf just east of the Pool of London. Watson and I surveyed her at anchor there last night and were defeated in attempting a closer inspection by the gates, chains and padlocks. Similar measures defeated our attempts to obtain an insight into the contents of the packing crates stored in the warehouse, again registered to your singular company, that adjoins her dock. Watson and I were definitely followed on our excursion, I expect by members of the same Royal Navy detail that you used to mount the operation against Sir Edward's study in Overstrand, probably against his house in Belgravia, and that you certainly use to crew the intriguing little fleet which operates behind the cover of your highly questionable business."

"Ostensibly this *business* appears to be no more sinister than fishing, and perhaps carrying out a little gentle trade with the Low Countries. But there is more to it, is there not, Mycroft? What is it, Mycroft? What are you engaged in? Smuggling? Smuggling weapons? Are *you* responsible for the fate of these missing vessels? Were they compromised in some way? You obviously knew from your contacts at the Admiralty and the Board of Trade" – here Holmes indicated Mr Churchill – "that there would be little difficulty in covering up the loss of two fishing boats which had seemingly gone to the bottom through natural disaster. The events would not be deemed significant enough to merit a Board enquiry or a hearing in the Admiralty court. And as, clearly, these vessels were crewed and probably sabotaged by Royal Navy personnel seconded to special operations, there would be no loss of life or bereaved families calling for inquests."

Holmes reached into the inside pocket of his waistcoat and withdrew three items. The first was the inflated photograph of our friend with the red birthmark upon his face, and the second was the telegram Holmes had received only that morning from Dartmouth. Holmes laid the photograph down upon Mycroft's desk and tapped it gently. "I first became acquainted with this gentleman as a Mr Caulfield. Watson and I later heard him referred to as a Mr Naylor. In fact he is Lieutenant Colin Boyes, late of the Royal Navy and now seconded to special duties in Whitehall. These duties clearly include acting as representative of the firm of Mendel & Newcombe with the Norfolk harbour authorities, and scattering stolen items once belonging to Sir Edward Muster across the criminal classes of the East End of London."

Holmes laid down the third item on the mahogany desk in front of him, next to the photograph of Boyes. It was the cryptic business card we had recovered from Marks' left luggage locker at Liverpool Street station.

"This belongs to another member of your personal militia. One Seaman Marks."

Holmes reached across and recovered the business card he had hurled dramatically upon the desk when we entered the study. He laid this card carefully alongside the one he had just extracted from his waistcoat. There was no address upon the latter. But in the bottom right hand corner of both cards a telephone number was printed in flowing black script. The legend 'Whitehall 821' was clearly visible on both. They matched.

"This is the card you gave me at the onset of this adventure, Mycroft," said Holmes softly, fingering the first. "And as you know, this was the telephone number I rang to set up our meeting today."

Holmes retreated to his chair and sat, arms folded and with a set frown of expectation.

It was Captain Cumming who spoke next. He looked briefly at Churchill and Mycroft before speaking. Wearing a monocle and resplendent in his uniform, Cumming looked every inch the professional naval officer.

"We had hoped to have you here today merely to offer our thanks and congratulations for breaking the Massner spy ring. The Prime Minister himself, Lord Asquith, has been informed, and is pleased. For myself, as one of the two chiefs of our recently created Secret Service Bureau, it is the work of men like Felix Massner and Gunther Haag that we are so desperately trying to counter during these tense times. You have done myself, and my department, a great favour. We now have access to some very interesting papers and records which will enable us to assess the full extent of the Massner spy ring. However, you have clearly uncovered a considerable amount of ... additional information during the course of your investigations."

Holmes and I waited patiently. There was silence for a moment, during which time the only sound to be heard was that of a blackbird, coming in through the window at the rear of the house.

Finally Mycroft sighed heavily, then looked both at Mr Churchill and Captain Cumming. They both nodded briefly.

"Very well," said Mycroft. "What you are about to hear will go with you to your graves. You are correct, Sherlock. My colleagues and I did retain your services to track down a spy, while at the same time having other matters in hand. I will now enlighten you on the final pieces of your jigsaw."

"There is a war coming with Germany. Oh, maybe not now, not today, not next week, not next month, and probably not next year. But sooner or later Great Britain will find herself at war with Imperial Germany and her allies on the continent. The underlying problem for the whole continent is that every European nation has so shackled itself with a complex network of alliances that it will take just one hostile incident and the whole continent will be ablaze. It is as inevitable as night following day. And we are receiving proof upon proof of the hostile intent within the Kaiser's Government."

Mycroft proceeded to elaborate in a measured fashion.

"The naval race in which we are engaged with the Germans shows no sign of abating, despite the recent efforts of our War Secretary, Lord Haldane, to reach terms with them. German spies are flooding into these islands to probe our strengths and weaknesses in the event of a German invasion. The Kaiser's cabinet is more or less openly pursuing a policy of encouraging unrest in Ireland, and is suspected of supplying arms to Irish Republicans. The colonial lobby in Berlin and the high German Imperialists are looking to flex their muscles against British Imperial possessions in Africa and elsewhere. And through reports reaching us from abroad, we have had an insight into the European invasion plans of the German General Staff, the so-called Schlieffen plan, which details how troops will smash through France, and in all likelihood Belgium and Luxembourg as well, on the way to the channel ports and possible invasion of England."

"And in the process openly violating the neutrality of the Low Countries?" queried Holmes.

Mycroft looked grim. "We believe so. Belgium and Luxembourg lie directly in the path of the German advance, and in any case it would make sound strategic sense for the Germans to occupy these two countries to protect their northern flank."

Mr Churchill interjected at this point.

"I have in my very hand a report compiled by a British engineer working in Luxembourg. This reached me in September last year. This man goes into great detail on the workings and sudden expansion of the German railway system, the increase in lines, and the rapid construction near the Belgian border of large military loading platforms, of such length that they can be easily used for the loading and unloading of troops. I quote directly; 'They (the Germans) are working at all points simultaneously so as to have done the bulk of the work next year with a view to having a complete set of strategic railways between the Belgian frontier on one side and the rivers Rhine and Moselle on the other.'"

"We know that this strategic expansion of the railways was begun six years ago," continued Mycroft. "So you see, we are working to prepare for the inevitable. Overtly you will have seen the signs in the creation of the Official Secrets Act last year, and in the moves to monitor foreign nationals under alien registration proposals. We have set up liaison offices between our own General Staff and their French counterparts, particularly following the Agadir Crisis of last year, when the Germans sent a gunboat to support anti-French demonstrations within French Morocco. Other preparations are, however, hidden from the public. Six years ago a secret committee was set up by Lord Fisher to draft naval plans to be used in the event of war. In 1909 we set up the Secret Service, with a mandate to investigate and identify German spies on these shores and to set up our own network of agents abroad. Clearly having our own intelligence network on the continent was perceived as vital in forewarning of the enemy's intentions."

"Last year I was recalled from retirement on the orders of the Prime Minister personally, who had had sight of some of my reports warning of German intentions. I was ordered to form a cabal with Mr Churchill, who shared my views, and Captain Cumming, who was at that time laying plans for the infiltration of the continent by his fledgling Secret Service organisation. We were tasked with identifying military, political and economic opportunities to gain any possible edge over Germany, to exploit any weakness that we could spot, and to identify and close any similar weakness in British policy or attitudes. In short my colleagues and I are engaged in a twilight war against Imperial Germany; we have a handful of trusted staff who look after all our clerical and administrative needs, and command a section of covert navy personnel, but we report only to the Prime Minister. Officially we do not exist, which is just as well. The work we are engaged in is, to put it mildly, suspect from the point of international law. I do not say that revelation of our existence could be the touchpaper that sends the continent into conflagration, but I do know that if we were found to exist it would put the British Government in a truly awkward position."

"One of our activities, however, combined with a unique set of circumstances at the beginning of this year, could have had very grave results. From the middle of last year, we have sought to expand upon Captain Cummings' activities in setting up spy networks in Europe by setting up an infrastructure designed to be of actual military and intelligence benefit in wartime. We sought to establish listening posts, safe houses, escape networks for British prisoners, train watching posts in border areas, suitable locations at which to send and receive smuggled information, and so on. We even sought to identify locations where we might house large quantities of military stores on the continent. In short, we sought to develop all the activities that might give us an advantage in wartime. We sought to set up this network principally in Holland, which was politically neutral, but more importantly was, as far as we could establish, likely to escape the German advance under the Schlieffen Plan. Moreover, much of the country borders Germany on its Eastern frontier."

"We thus set up two methods of conveying essential *materiel* ... radios, communications and signalling equipment, small quantities of arms and explosives ... to Holland. These routes, as you found out, involved using small boats to smuggle equipment from a Norfolk creek and the Thames estuary to The Hague, where our people on the other side would disperse it. Unfortunately we have discovered to our cost that The Hague is crawling with our opposite numbers in the German intelligence apparatus, led by a wily fox named Gustav Steinhauer, a former private detective."

"I encountered him during the case of the *St. Petersburg Deception*," murmured Holmes.

"Quite," continued Mycroft. "Well, we discovered recently that two of our vessels had come under suspicion of clandestine operations. To explain this in context, I need to cover another subject first. You have said that, in your recent researches, you came across references to the International Opium Conference in The Hague, which took place between December and January, and Sir Edward Muster's role in that conference."

Holmes replied, "I discovered that Sir Edward was reluctant to discuss this conference, which he admitted he had attended, and I suspected that he fought against any legislative clauses involving cocaine because they may have damaged his own business interests in the international pharmaceuticals market. But clearly there was more to it."

"Quite," replied Mycroft, dryly. "We will return to that in a moment. Prior to Sir Edward's arrival in The Hague in January, however, the conference in question had already turned most unpleasant. I confess that myself and my colleagues here were taken aback at the vitriol that ran forth from this conference, which we initially believed would be no more than an exercise in lip-service to its American sponsors. However, the German delegation actively pursued a policy of forcing the abandonment of the opium trade, an initiative that would have had considerable economic repercussions for us. We planned to fight back by recommending measures against the cocaine trade, which would have hurt the Germans in a similar manner."

"Why was this conference convened in the first place?" I asked.

Mycroft sighed. "The intention of the Americans, who sponsored the conference, was to force the thirteen participating countries, through international legislation, to abandon the trade in opium and its main derivatives, morphine and heroin, save that which was legitimately required for *bona fide* pharmaceutical purposes. You must both be aware that the global market for these drugs far exceeds the amounts required for medicinal purposes; the overwhelming majority of demand is, tragically, addiction-driven. It is a bald fact that all the European powers are complicit in a very lucrative business that is little more than a trade in human misery in the Middle and Far East. But I digress. The reasons for the Americans sponsoring this conference were twofold; they were responding to a genuine anti-drugs crusade within the United States of America, a movement that has gained momentum on the back of the wider movement for the prohibition of alcohol, but they also sought to strangle our opium trade with China, as the Chinese economy was staggering under the enormous amounts of money paid to Britain for our opium exports to that country; not to mention the sizeable percentage of the Chinese workforce rendered incapable due to opium addiction. Their second motive was, therefore, not entirely philanthropic; the Americans want an economically strong China as a market for their own products."

"In any case, the Germans were only too delighted to support the Americans in their quest to ban opium trading, realising the value of this commodity to the British Imperial economy. In reply the British delegation, under the secret direction of this cabal, introduced cocaine onto the agenda and proposed that if opium was to be banned, the same restrictions be applied to cocaine. The scourge of cocaine is no

162

less than that of opium and its derivatives, but again, the Germans are making enormous amounts of money from this trade; they are also quite happily smuggling the drug into British India and Burma. The Americans have their own problems with domestic cocaine addiction, so it was fairly easy for us to table its inclusion."

"Are these drugs of such importance to the respective economies of the two countries?" enquired Sherlock.

"You would be surprised. We went to war with China to protect our opium trade in 1858. Over twenty per cent of the entire economy of British India is accounted for in profits from the opium trade. As recently as five years ago over fifty per cent of the taxes of British Malaya came from opium trading. And on the other side of the water, cocaine is to Germany what opium, morphine and heroin are to Britain. Cocaine, via legitimate domestic production and production for export onto the world market, accounts for a huge amount of their gross domestic product. In effect, introducing cocaine onto the agenda at The Hague was a *quid pro quo* by us, a direct *riposte* to the morphine gambit initiated by the Germans. In effect, this was a form of economic warfare conducted under the aegis of the twilight war I spoke of earlier. We do not want to be forced into a position where we are going to lose our drugs revenue, but if the worst comes to the worst, we are certainly going to ensure that the Germans are similarly disadvantaged."

"And how in Heaven's name does this relate to the smuggling operation you and your colleagues are running, and the loss of those fishing boats?" I asked in astonishment.

Mycroft held up his hand.

"I have explained that we were initially taken aback by the vehemence of the Germans in working against us at this conference. It was not long before we authorised the interception of the German diplomatic bag leaving their embassy in London for Berlin." He smiled. "Contrary to suspicions among the international diplomatic community this sort of thing is not done as a matter of course. However in this case we wanted to gather any intelligence available regarding the German perceptions of the British political stance and attitude to events in The Hague as they were unfolding. I must confess that in this regard we learnt little. However, in due course we caught an altogether different fish in our net."

Mycroft consulted some notes on a black leather binder in front of him on his desk.

"By the beginning of February the Opium Conference had come to an end with no firm results. By introducing our cocaine proposal we stalled and slowed proceedings so that no agreement was reached ... as we hoped would be the case. But the national mood on both sides of the water was nasty, ugly ... the British were accused of being wreckers by the German press, who took the moral high ground. Our newspapers retorted in kind. The repercussions of this conference again raised the simmering tensions between ourselves and Germany that had subsided briefly following the Agadir scare of last year. I continued to authorise the interception of the diplomatic bag for the short term."

"Then on ... the 10th of February, I authorised an operation involving one of our boats, the *Yarmouth Adventuress* ... against my better judgement, I have to say, given the atmosphere in The Hague at the time. She was due to drop off some equipment at The Hague where our people on the other side would disperse it as normal. But somehow our opposite numbers in the German Intelligence Service had got wind of the operation. Dutch port authority officials, accompanied by German embassy staff, moved to impound her in The Hague's Scheveningen harbour. God only knows what the results would have been if this had happened and she was searched. Fortunately a Dutch friend of ours tipped off her captain and she was able to make her escape into open water, minutes ahead of the boarding party."

"This incident gave us all" – Mycroft indicated his colleagues – "a scare. There was no question of us using this boat or another we had used over the past six months, the *Misty Jane*, again. As far as we knew both had been fatally compromised. Hostile propaganda, or worse, an excuse for war, could have been the result if they were exposed to the enemy again. To ensure this could never be a possibility, we decided to destroy the vessels. As she moved into open water on that fateful day the *Yarmouth Adventuress* made contact by wireless with a Royal Navy warship that was in the area. I authorised her immediate sinking in international waters. The warship sent her to the bottom after taking off the crew. The *Misty Jane* was destroyed the next day by a time-delayed explosive charge that gave the appearance of a fire off Blakeney Point. The two crew, Royal Navy men as you now know, got away and came ashore further down the coast."

"Why did you leave your other vessels untouched?" I queried suddenly.

It was Holmes who answered. "Because this group had only recently bought them, and, I suspect, they had not yet made a clandestine visit to The Hague, with the consequent possibility of identification. I discovered their acquisition details during my researches yesterday."

Mycroft nodded. "That is correct. Nevertheless our smuggling policy is currently under review and will certainly be wound down until further notice. The *Pearl* and *Lindisfarne* will soon have a discreet change of ownership and Mendel & Newcombe will be disbanded. The *Lindisfarne* was being made fast to the quay last night when you two mounted your night-time surveillance of her in the pool of London." He smiled. "One of my men followed you to ensure you did not cause any more trouble. I must also apologise for the behaviour of Marks when he attacked you in Blakeney. My team are all somewhat sensitive to snoopers, and he simply did not recognise you in the gloom."

I nodded but Holmes merely grunted.

"Following the revelation that the *Yarmouth Adventuress* had been compromised, my colleagues and I were prepared to believe that it was simply good intelligence work on the part of the enemy. It certainly made us think. But then, as I have hinted, our diplomatic bag surveillance bore fruit in a most unexpected way. On the 15th of February we recovered from the bag an item that was clearly a spy's report and we were able to make a rapid copy of the text before sending the original on its way. It was couched in a rudimentary code that we quickly broke. I must say that there was little of real intelligence value therein but the writer was an agent, code-named Raven, who was clearly situated in North Norfolk. There were references to comings and goings at Weybourne army camp, for example. And more importantly there were references to the identity of two fishing boats that Mr Churchill here had used in the past to bring him ashore at Overstrand; namely the *Yarmouth Adventuress* and the *Misty Jane*. Although as you rightly said earlier, Sherlock, my colleague here used this novelty form of transport as a whim, the fact was that they were our special operations boats which were normally engaged in highly sensitive work and crewed by members of our very own covert Navy detail."

"We suspected that this spy had been reporting to Berlin on a regular basis," continued Mycroft.

"He had," murmured Holmes dryly. "Possibly six times a year for the past decade ..."

"As I say," Mycroft went on with a glance at his brother, "we suspected that this was merely one of a sequence of similar reports issuing from Norfolk and finding their way to Berlin during previous months when we did not have the diplomatic bag covered. If these previous reports also contained references to the two vessels and Mr Churchill's personal use of the same, there was every chance that Steinhauer may well have made a connection between their continued association with Mr Churchill here, a known political 'War Hawk', and their frequent appearance on the continent in The Hague. Steinhauer's agents keep a close watch on foreign shipping in The Hague and it is now clear that the *Yarmouth Adventuress*, at least, and very possibly the *Misty Jane* as well, had been marked. It is entirely possible that the wily fox was privy to further intelligence on the other side of the water which served to reinforce his suspicions; we now have to consider the possibility, for example, that some of our activities in the Dutch interior have been compromised and the trail has been traced back to The Hague."

"I do believe that Steinhauer treated the intelligence contained in the Norfolk reports seriously, particularly regarding the connection between these fishing vessels and yourself, Mr Churchill," observed Holmes. "I know that Massner attempted to contact Sir Daniel Everard on Thursday the 15th of February, at which time he would have only recently taken delivery of Sir Daniel's last report from his intermediary in London, Haag, and forwarded it on to Germany via the German Embassy; the very report, clearly, that your cabal intercepted on the same day on its way to Berlin. I would be very surprised if Massner had not received urgent instructions from Steinhauer to discover all he could regarding the fishing vessels in question and your interest in them, particularly in light of the dramatic events in The Hague that Mycroft has just recounted. Steinhauer himself would not have received Sir Daniel's last report of the 10th of February until the very end of last week at best, but, as you say, Mycroft, if previous reports had already contained similar references to these fishing vessels then his suspicions could already have been aroused either late last year, or early this year."

"I infer, then, that you believed Sir Edward Muster to be the spy in question in North Norfolk?" Holmes asked Mycroft.

Mycroft nodded. "Although the evidence against Sir Edward was always circumstantial, he did seem to fit the bill. References in the report we intercepted to the British luminaries that reside, seasonally or otherwise, in Overstrand, placed the spy, as we saw it, firmly in that village. Sir Edward himself had only moved to Overstrand the previous autumn ..."

"... when Sea Marge was completed ..." interjected Holmes.

"... and coinciding with the formation of this group and our commencement of operations on the continent," Mycroft continued. "On account of his social status he moved in the same exalted circles as were accurately portrayed in the report; some of them key persons in the British political and business community. We greatly feared the damage he could do to us, or indeed could already have done to us, if he was indeed a German spy, and this angst on our part was compounded by the fact that the British Government had already used him in the past as a trusted ambassador to the Kaiser."

"There was one further factor guiding our belief that Sir Edward could be our man. Basically our suspicions regarding Sir Edward's character and motives had already been aroused some time before we intercepted this intelligence report from Overstrand. From the 6th of January Sir Edward joined the German delegation at the International Opium Conference in The Hague and spoke elegantly and forcefully against the cocaine proposal. He also spoke with zeal in favour of the morphine gambit, a fact that surprised our own secret observer at the conference. Our observer reported back that he feared that Muster might be following the programme of another German agency, rather than merely defending his own business interests. With the benefit of hindsight, this observation may have been tinged with a touch of paranoia inspired by the tense climate of the conference. However, we were concerned enough at the time to place one of our people in his office to make some discreet enquiries on our behalf, while ostensibly working as a bicycle courier."

"I presume by *business interests* your are referring to his interests in pharmaceuticals?" I asked.

Mycroft nodded. "The German cocaine apparatus consists of ten enormous pharmaceutical companies centred around Darmstadt and Frankfurt, the largest one being Merck. Our latest figures show us that Merck produced nearly forty tons of pure cocaine for export in 1910 ... over 75% of Germany's entire output onto the world market. You knew from your research, Sherlock, that Sir Edward had interests in pharmaceuticals; what you were perhaps less cognisant of was that he is a sleeping partner on Merck's board of directors. I must confess the extent of his business interests in cocaine has only been revealed to us over the last few days as we went deeper into his business interests." He shrugged. "I now surmise he was willing to take the stand against us for humanitarian reasons in denouncing our opium and morphine trades, but was sufficiently self-interested to defend his own concerns in the cocaine trade robustly."

"Of course, at the time we intercepted this intelligence report we did not have all the facts of his business interests and other detailed pertinent information at our fingertips. I quickly authorised the attempts against his homes, which, as you discovered, were carried out in Norfolk by the Navy personnel operating for us along that coast. Likewise our Navy men also carried out the operation in Belgravia, but as you discovered, we had the wrong man. Sir Daniel Everard was the spy in question."

"Haag and Massner," began Holmes accusingly. "Was it your intention to murder them to ensure their silence, or did you fear the publicity of a trial for treason?"

Mycroft held out his hands in protestation. "Of course not! Honestly, Sherlock, the men who went to arrest Haag went to detain him in all good faith. But he produced a pistol and opened fired on them. They were both forced to return fire in self-defence and Haag was killed."

"And Massner?"

"We hoped to avoid a repetition of the Haag incident, which unfortunately occurred in broad daylight and attracted the attentions of half the East End. Thanks to your tip, Sherlock, we identified Massner as the user of that mysterious Post Office box in Oxford Street. It was short work to discover that he was a translator in the Foreign Office, and to discover his address. Special Branch men under my control went to his house after dark the night before last. Unfortunately, the debacle was almost a repeat of the Haag 'arrest'. My men were forced to kill Massner in self-defence."

"Does your reach extend into all areas of the Government?" I asked in wonder.

Mycroft shook his head. "Very few Government officials even know of our existence. As I have said, we report directly to the Prime Minister's office. The cabal includes we three sitting in this room, a handful of clerical staff, and a Royal Navy detachment. We can also call on a detail of Special Branch officers when required. As you suspected, Sherlock, Carlisle and his men were working for me, as were the officers who went to arrest Haag and Massner. It would be wrong to suggest we are omnipotent. That said, if I wish to make certain things happen in officialdom, such as stalling an enquiry into the sinking of a fishing boat, for example, I can usually make it happen. The investigations launched by Inspectors Jackson and Terry, for example, will quietly be shelved, and as you suspected, Sherlock, the Massner and Haag shootings will indeed remain unsolved. By the way, I'll take the Everard documents now."

Holmes handed over the documents we had recovered from The Gables in Overstrand.

"How did you research Sir Edward Muster's routine, and the geography of his houses, prior to conducting your raids?" asked Holmes.

"Halkin Place proved to be a reasonably straightforward infiltration, due to the design of the house, and the fact that the Muster family was not in residence at the time. One quick scouting trip was all it took and we were in a position to conduct the operation."

Mycroft rolled his eyes in disbelief. "I must say that I never authorised our people to remove actual items from Halkin Place to make the motive look like robbery. That ridiculous idea was thought of during the actual event by one of the fools who conducted the operation. He has since been severely disciplined as a result. Once we were in possession of the material I had no idea what to do with it. Eventually, as you discovered, we concluded that the best plan was to disperse the goods into the more shady parts of the East End to at least give the lie that a robbery for gain had been carried out. Perhaps fortunately, nothing of real value was taken."

"We knew about the general layout of Sir Edward's house in Norfolk because, of course, Mr Churchill here was acquainted with the place from his summers holidaying in the village. That operation was a near-run thing. Our men mounted a tedious night vigil in Sea Marge gardens waiting for the most opportune moment to strike. They infiltrated the gardens on foot from the beach when the tide was out. When they were disturbed in the study, the water was only an hour or so away from high tide. Our men had to escape along the shore with the receding tide still pulling at their ankles."

"Ah," said Holmes. "I thought that was how it was done."

My friend looked across at me, and then back to his brother. "I have only one final question," he continued. "If you were unwilling to confide in me the full facts surrounding this case at the outset, why did you engage my services at all?"

Mycroft sighed again. "It was my decision to engage you, Sherlock. I desperately wanted your expertise in conclusively identifying the Norfolk spy, and I knew you would not fail me in this regard. Personally I wanted to lay all the facts surrounding this business before you, including making a clean breast of our clandestine activities, but the Prime Minister was reluctant for me to do so, fearing that the greater number of people that knew about our operations, the greater the chance that they would be compromised. I can sympathise with his point of view; if our activities are ever officially unmasked, it will be he and his office that will have to deal with the European repercussions of this business. The stakes are terribly high, Sherlock. There was every chance that Gustav Steinhauer had identified our boats engaged in illegal smuggling operations in the very city where a major international conference, with all its tensions and ramifications, was taking place."

"I admit, however, that it must seem silly that I had to keep these details from you of all people, Sherlock, when you have acted for the Government on several occasions previously. Nevertheless, I had to respect the Prime Minister's directive; he is an obstinate man and would not change his mind on this once he was decided, despite my warning him that you would in all likelihood discover the secrets of Mendel & Newcombe off your own bat. As it is my colleagues and I will have to advise the Prime Minister that this is indeed the case, but that you and Dr Watson will not breathe a word of the matter and have been sworn to silence."

"There was one further advantage, in my eyes, in retaining your services. You are still a household name in detection. If Sir Edward Muster was by chance an innocent man, he can only have been reassured that the British Government was taking such a serious interest in his welfare by engaging the great Sherlock Holmes ... with any luck it would have helped disarm any suspicions he may have harboured that he himself was the actual target of our enquiries. I also hoped that by engaging you in such a public manner a message would be sent to any German agencies that might be watching that as far as the British authorities were concerned, Sir Edward was above suspicion. To this end I let slip details of your involvement to certain national and local newspapers in the county of Norfolk, through an intermediary of course. This resulted in some ... garish headlines that broadcast your involvement in no uncertain fashion."

"Of course!" I exclaimed. "The headlines in the Sunday newspapers." I remembered Holmes' chagrin as he noted the lead articles in *The Times* and *Daily Mail* while at breakfast in the long hall of Sea Marge the previous weekend. After all that had happened, it seemed a lifetime ago.

"Remarkable," muttered Holmes. I could tell that his nose had been put firmly out of joint by the morning's revelations.

Mycroft now changed tack in an effort to mollify his brother.

"It is ironic, Sherlock, is it not, that opium should again have played such an important part in this case, as it did in 1900 when we sent you to China to investigate the fate of our missing diplomat?"

I looked over at Holmes, startled. This was one case of which I was not aware.

Holmes smiled at me. "You must forgive me, Watson. Over the course of our long and rewarding association there have been a few times when the Government has called on my services, usually using Mycroft as its mouthpiece, to lend assistance in particularly sensitive international entanglements. I have taken it upon myself to investigate these affairs alone, unwilling to risk injury to you, my oldest friend, in some madcap venture abroad. However, since

Mycroft has raised it in this forum, I can confirm that I undertook an assignment to Shanghai in 1900 to investigate some peculiar events during the so-called Boxer Rebellion. During parts of 1903 and 1904 I was in France as an observer of the damage done to the Third Republic by the Dreyfuss affair; through contacts of mine I attempted to halt the negative view of France, that of a country in natural decay and a state of weakness, being perceived in the German embassy in Paris and communicated back to Berlin. In 1907 I was in St. Petersburg, tracing a saboteur attempting to wreck the Anglo-Russian Entente. And this year I have betrayed my previous reservations and drawn your good self into this national security business. I must confess that this affair has been the most *outré* of all, if only" – here Holmes cast another withering look at Mycroft – "because the investigating detectives were only supplied with finite information at the outset of the enquiry."

Mycroft sighed. "The correct result has been attained, Sherlock. For any personal sense of affront, let me offer my apologies. This is the end, gentlemen," said Mycroft with an air of finality. "Thank you! Please remember that these events never officially took place, and never speak of them to anyone."

Holmes bowed stiffly. We took our leave and were shown to the door by the immaculately dressed doorman.

"A glass of beer in Mayfair would be rather pleasant, Watson, would it not? Let us retrace our steps across the park."

The sun was shining as we left Queen Anne's Gate.

"You must let me have the details of the three investigations you just mentioned for my case files," I remonstrated.

Holmes shook his head wearily, and then gave me an exasperated grin.

"One day, Watson, one day!"

We carried on across the park towards Mayfair.

Epilogue

The title for these extraordinary events, suggested by me in a flippant moment, came to stick, and a small clique of British mandarins ever after referred to the events of February 1912 as the 'Morphine Gambit'. Hopefully within these pages my readers can appreciate now the full reasons why the British delegation introduced cocaine onto the agenda of the International Opium Conference at The Hague in 1911-1912. At the time this move was met with considerable surprise, and there was much speculation in the European newspapers at the British motive for doing so; little can anyone have known of the true story of espionage and conspiracy that lay beneath. At the conclusion of the first International Opium Conference a second was planned by the American organisers for the following year, and Mycroft's group would prepare for another tense summit; in the event however, the second conference failed to convene as Europe began to slide irreversibly towards world war.

Holmes was recalled to assist his country once more, to my knowledge. On the eve of war, in August 1914, Holmes finally unmasked the top German spy in this country, Von Bork. It was the culmination of his work in unravelling the German spy network that he began in East Anglia in 1912.

Mycroft's agency succeeded in burying the evidence of their activities along the English coast, and in Holland. By a tragic coincidence the organisation which may have been in a position to ask some awkward questions, namely the Board of Trade, was shortly to become wholly diverted by the desperate events surrounding the sinking of the *Titanic* in the North Atlantic.

Sir Edward Muster fared badly in the aftermath of the affair. To my knowledge he never had an inkling of what really went on at Overstrand that February, nor of the circumstances surrounding, but he fell foul of a suspicious Winston Churchill. Churchill, a fine man with many good qualities, never quite overcame his paranoia that Muster had learnt or guessed something of the Mendel & Newcombe business. Sir Edward became besieged by anti-German sentiment and his business and private lives suffered. Rumours began that he was indeed a German spy; that he was preparing a bridgehead for invading German troops at Overstrand, and was signalling to German submarines offshore from the top floor of Sea Marge. Whether these rumours fed Churchill's paranoia, or whether the Secret Service, with or without his knowledge, spread these rumours to discredit Sir Edward, is open to question. Certainly at the outbreak of war Churchill had Muster arrested as an enemy alien. Sir Edward was stripped of his knighthood and shortly after was deported to America. For me the treatment of Sir Edward was the saddest part of the whole affair, and happened despite Mycroft's pleading clemency for his friend.

Mycroft went on to direct Secret Service operations during

the Great War, using those very same networks begun in 1912. From Holland his people infiltrated prisoner of war and refugee camps in Belgium and Germany to gain vital battle intelligence. His agents aided escaping prisoners of war and manned train watching posts along the German-Dutch border to gain information on enemy troop movements. And those same drugs that had been to the fore during those exciting events of 1912 raised their collectively ugly heads once again. Showing the ruthless side of him that I had only seen once or twice, he capitalised upon the German soldier's weakness for heroin, morphine and cocaine. His agents used these drugs mercilessly to bribe German sentries on the Dutch border; as a result, all manner of information and material passed unhindered both ways across the border, all to the benefit of the allied cause. It was as he had made clear to me on that unforgettable morning in Queen Anne's Gate in 1912; cocaine and heroin were weapons, on both tactical and strategic levels. Not for nothing was morphine addiction known as 'The Army Disease'. It made Holmes' experiences with cocaine during the late nineteenth century seem positively innocent by comparison.

I retired to Rye in 1913 but served in a limited capacity during the Great War. Following the war I wrote up the few cases of Holmes' which had still escaped me – among them the *Morphine Gambit*, the *Shanghai Sorcerer Mystery* and the *St. Petersburg Deception*.

Dr John H. Watson, M.D.
Rye.
November, 1920.

A Final Note

Some readers may be interested to learn that much of the adventure you have just read is based on fact. Indeed the property of Sea Marge does exist in Overstrand and has a somewhat similar history to that given in this book.

The Sea Marge was built in 1908 as a country retreat by Sir Edgar Speyer, a German banker. He used his wealth to satisfy tastes in interior design that were eclectic even by the standards of the day. Hand-painted delft tiles adorned walls, Adam fireplaces were installed and a fine minstrels' gallery constructed.

Unfortunately Sir Edgar did not long enjoy his investment. As a friend of the Kaiser, he became the object of much suspicion with the onset of World War I. There were even rumours that the Sea Marge was used as a vantage point for signalling to German submarines. He was stripped of his knighthood and British citizenship and eventually deported.

His fine house stood abandoned and empty until 1935 when it began a flourishing period as a hotel, numbering Winston Churchill among its regular guests. From 1955 to 1990 the benefits of sea air led to the Sea Marge operating as a nursing home.

It was then privately purchased but the new owner could not maintain the house and it deteriorated through neglect, theft and vandalism.

Fortunately, the Sea Marge was rescued by the Mackenzie family, lovingly restored and reopened as a hotel in 1996. A stolen fireplace was tracked down to Northampton and returned to pride of place in the reception.

Most of the minstrels' gallery had been destroyed but one surviving panel was used as the inspiration for the stunning replica that can be seen today.

If ever in the area you would certainly be made most welcome at this country-style hotel located on the cliffs at Overstrand.

Sherlock Holmes will return
in a new adventure

Sherlock Holmes
and the
Mayfair Murders

by

David Britland

"With five volumes you could fill that gap on that second shelf"
(Sherlock Holmes, *The Empty House*)

So why not collect all 40 murder mysteries from Breese Books at just £7.50 each?
Available from all good bookshops, or direct from the publisher with free UK postage
& packing. Alternatively you can get full details of all our publications, including our
range of audio books, and order on-line where you can also join our mailing list and
see our latest special offers.

MYSTERY OF A HANSOM CAB
SHERLOCK HOLMES AND THE ABBEY SCHOOL MYSTERY
SHERLOCK HOLMES AND THE ADLER PAPERS
SHERLOCK HOLMES AND THE BAKER STREET DOZEN
SHERLOCK HOLMES AND THE BOULEVARD ASSASSIN
SHERLOCK HOLMES AND THE CHILFORD RIPPER
SHERLOCK HOLMES AND THE CHINESE JUNK AFFAIR
SHERLOCK HOLMES AND THE CIRCUS OF FEAR
SHERLOCK HOLMES AND THE DISAPPEARING PRINCE
SHERLOCK HOLMES AND THE DISGRACED INSPECTOR
SHERLOCK HOLMES AND THE EGYPTIAN HALL ADVENTURE
SHERLOCK HOLMES AND THE FRIGHTENED GOLFER
SHERLOCK HOLMES AND THE GIANT'S HAND
SHERLOCK HOLMES AND THE GREYFRIARS SCHOOL MYSTERY
SHERLOCK HOLMES AND THE HAMMERFORD WILL
SHERLOCK HOLMES AND THE HOLBORN EMPORIUM
SHERLOCK HOLMES AND THE HOUDINI BIRTHRIGHT
SHERLOCK HOLMES AND THE LONGACRE VAMPIRE
SHERLOCK HOLMES AND THE MAN WHO LOST HIMSELF
SHERLOCK HOLMES AND THE SANDRINGHAM HOUSE MYSTERY
SHERLOCK HOLMES AND THE SECRET MISSION
SHERLOCK HOLMES AND THE SECRET SEVEN
SHERLOCK HOLMES AND THE TANDRIDGE HALL MYSTERY
SHERLOCK HOLMES AND THE TELEPHONE MURDER MYSTERY
SHERLOCK HOLMES AND THE THEATRE OF DEATH
SHERLOCK HOLMES AND THE THREE POISONED PAWNS
SHERLOCK HOLMES AND THE TITANTIC TRAGEDY
SHERLOCK HOLMES AND THE TOMB OF TERROR
SHERLOCK HOLMES AND THE YULE-TIDE MYSTERY
SHERLOCK HOLMES: A DUEL WITH THE DEVIL
SHERLOCK HOLMES AT THE RAFFLES HOTEL
SHERLOCK HOLMES AT THE VARIETIES
SHERLOCK HOLMES ON THE WESTERN FRONT
SHERLOCK HOLMES: THE GHOST OF BAKER STREET
SPECIAL COMMISSION
THE ELEMENTARY CASES OF SHERLOCK HOLMES
THE TORMENT OF SHERLOCK HOLMES
THE TRAVELS OF SHERLOCK HOLMES
WATSON'S LAST CASE

Baker Street Studios Limited, Endeavour House, 170 Woodland Road,
Sawston, Cambridge CB22 3DX
www.breesebooks.com, sales@breesebooks.com